Cherished by You

THE FOUND BY YOU SERIES: BOOK FIVE

VICTORIA H SMITH

One

ROXIE

A light illuminated the cab, my awareness going off with that first flash. Another followed, and then another and my head rushed at the influx. Even though expected, they shocked the system. They always did.

Tense, I held my arms, watching as photographers piled on top of each other. They climbed, clawing over the most aggressive who'd made their way to the front of the pack. Those few got the first uninterrupted shots, what I knew to be nothing but tinted windows captured by their active shutters.

I swallowed, trying to breathe. The beading of my violet gown gave me something else to focus on as the limo came to a stop.

I patted around one with my fingertip, following the weaving strand. It swooped and turned, ending in a line just across my stomach. I held my hand there, sighing, feeling, and a larger hand slid between mine and the dress.

Griffin's fingers laced through mine, my own digits finding every space and groove between his wide ones. He squeezed, his other hand coming to rest on my neck, and using the tip of his thumb, he lifted my chin.

A flare of blue was what I got to see first, ocean-esque and calm in their gaze. His jaw relaxed, Griffin's mouth turned up in the corner, the freckle near the V of his upper lip moving with his smile.

"Nervous?" he asked, closing the space and touching our foreheads together. I felt every ounce of his warmth.

"Mmmhmm." The word breathed through my lips, my nerves a simmering cesspool. "Very."

The pads of his fingertips brushed across my neck, and then followed his lips. His mouth was warm and covered mine in everything that was ever wonderful.

Sighing, I fingered his collar, wanting to melt into him, wanting him to melt into me. Using our laced fingers, he brought me closer, nearly on his lap, and the swell of my breasts pressed firmly to his chest.

His taste consumed me, the smell of his aftershave surrounding me, and I let him take me to a far off place, one of him and his comfort. All too soon, he was the only thing. He was always the only thing.

"Just me and you," he said, pressing a kiss, and then another. He mouthed my jaw. "Only us, Roxie. No need for the fear. I'm with you always."

I closed my eyes, understanding with my nod. He told me to focus on him. I would focus on him, and I wouldn't be afraid.

"Only us," I told him, pulling away, and when I did, I got a final kiss, one in which he turned my cheek in the direction of his lips.

The door of our limo opened, and by my hand, he took me out into the fray, his six-foot-six inch frame covered in a black suit. It fit him in all the ways a suit should fit a man, close at his thighs and tapered at his long waist. The jacket stretched over his broad shoulders and wide chest, and he turned, revealing his flaxen hair smoothed back for tonight. Griffin Chandler... he was beautiful.

He brought me to him by my hands and then placed one on his arm.

The paparazzi surrounded us.

The minute we hit the red carpet, they took their position directly in front, and Griffin's people were the only thing holding them back. His name sounded in high alarm, the point guard for Miami a popular photo opportunity, and though Griffin responded to them, he never left me. As he said in the car, he was always with me.

He held me, positioning me with him while they took their photos, and they loved him for every ounce of attention he gave. They loved him.

Over four years of what I had. Over four years of being Griffin's wife and part of his world, and each time he amazed me. He allowed them to take photos like this was the first time, gave them his patience, and then left them like he couldn't wait to see them again. This man was a rarity, magnificent.

After the last round, we went to head down the rest of the red carpet, but then my name was said. In fact, they chanted it. They chanted: "Roxie!"

"What are you wearing?" came at me. "Show us the back of the gown, Roxie! It's gorgeous!" came more, and I did, my mouth a bit agape at the attention.

Griffin's fingers loosened from mine, but he didn't let go. He simply extended me over to them, and their attention with a smile on his face, and I posed in front of the stamped board, trying not to be overwhelmed as the photographers captured the silky train of my purple gown. After a few seconds, Griffin placed me back on his arm, and that's when something else shouted my way.

"Congratulations on your achievement, Roxie!" they said to me, and my heart well...

It swelled.

~

The lights in the wide auditorium dimmed later that night, the attendees of the awards ceremony zeroing in on a single presenter. So much had happened tonight, so many celebrities and pop stars both presenting and earning awards. I used to watch the ceremony at home from my couch. The BET Awards were big everywhere, even in my small neighborhood. I enjoyed getting to see the glitz and glamor while so far away, the flashing lights and star power. Never in my life did I think one day I'd be here.

Nor have anyone acknowledge me.

The presenter's lips moved, and I zoned out, watching as the second African American woman to ever win Best Actress directed the audience's attention to the massive side screens in the room.

"She's chair of the *Chandler Foundation*," she said, "an organization she founded with her husband and business partner, Griffin Chandler, which has provided the advancement of after-school programs to inner-city youth. These programs have kept children off the streets, and the organization itself has sent over a hundred young black women and men to college."

The audience applauded, the actress letting them with her pause, and I forgot to breathe. I forgot to think, everything.

I braced my hands on the armrests of my chair, my entire body shaking, but an arm coming around my shoulders lessened the quake, and the depth of a Texan drawl surrounded me in tranquility.

"You're okay," Griffin said, rubbing my shoulder. "You're fine. I'm proud of you."

He was proud of me.

I looked up at the presenter, trying to keep the anxiety in. The camera was on me at that time, my reaction on the screen.

You can do this. You can.

"She's done so much," the actress went on, tilting her head. Even from there, I could feel her eyes on me. I could feel everyone's eyes on me.

"But she still finds the time," she said, pointing at the room. "She's still there for any rising athlete or bright-eyed kid who hasn't even thought that far yet, for a personal meet up or even a midnight phone call to discuss their futures. Her consulting firm has matched dozens of professional athletes to respectable industry professionals all over the country, and that was only in her first few months post law school. The future is only bright for this girl, and let me tell you what, Roxie, the world can't wait to see what you do next. I present this ceremony's Humanitarian Award to Ms. Roxie Chandler!"

Her applause had everyone standing up, but the first, the very first, was my husband.

Griffin's applause boomed, leading the standing ovation, and I think that's what got to me.

My eyes watering, I couldn't breathe, and I reached up so far to hug him, his wingspan engulfing me in the best way.

"Go get your award, baby," he said to me, pressing a kiss to my mouth before wiping a thumb underneath my eye.

I nodded, his hand on my back as I turned toward the aisle. But before I could make it out, I received yet more warm hugs.

Kerry Donavan squeezed me, my friend and confidante since coming to the crazy excitement of this town. Her own husband transferred teams, passing down the torch to mine long ago. The Donavans had been family friends of the Chandlers since the beginning, and I had a feeling for many years to come.

"Get it, girl," she said, giving me one last full body hug before letting me out. Her husband, Kendrick, wrapped a brief hug around me as well, wishing me his congratulations on the other side of her.

Somehow, someway, I made my way to the front, the silk of my gown hiked in my hands. My vision blurry, every step I took was shaky, and an attendant had to help me up the stairs in the wide room.

The actress came forward, taking my hand to lead me the rest of the way. Together, we made it to the podium, and she handed me something insane.

She handed me an award.

My name was embossed in gold lettering on a plate at the bottom of a glass statuette, its crystal hands reaching toward the sky. So heavy, the actress helped me take it back to the podium, laughing a little while she hugged me and said congratulations. After a pat on the back, she left the spotlight. I faced the audience, the moment such a blur. I think I heard my name. I think I heard congratulations, but I know I heard him. I heard Griffin out there amongst the crowd. Perhaps, because I was looking at him, his large frame stood out from the many as I watched him cup his mouth and call out to me between rounds of applause. Eventually, he lowered his hands, using just his mouth.

"Only us," he mouthed, and I read him all too clearly. We'd talked to each other that way so many times before. He was right. It was only us, but soon, we'd make that even better.

I breathed, moving into the mic. "Thank you."

More applause and I covered my mouth, the experience so much to take in.

Bracing the podium, I concentrated on blue eyes, my rock.

I parted my lips. "You all have been so supportive of me and *Chandler Foundation*."

Sniffing, I had to collect myself for a moment, thinking

about all those financial contributions, that *support,* and positivity I got for my little dream. I wanted to do something with my education, help people, and the ones in my community allowed me to do that. The connections Griffin made over the years garnered initial influence, but many, if not all, pushed on with me well past the life of their financial donations. Together, we made the *Foundation* happen, and I was grateful for each one of them.

I braced the stand. "We're all together in this. We're *all* helping to get these kids in school and keep them there."

I got a breath in during another round of support, more applause.

"I'm just a girl, a woman from Wisconsin," I said, shaking my head at that. "I'm a woman who met a man and found her everything in every way and all at once, and I thank him so much for that. I thank him for his love, and I thank him for his constant support."

I found him in the audience then, smiling at me as he always did.

"Griffin..." I said, swallowing. "Griffin, I love you. I love you so much."

The applause went out to him this time. He deserved that much and more.

His hands to his mouth, Griffin kissed his fingertips, opening them out to me in response.

"Every day I look at my life and wonder how I got so lucky," I said, not breaking eye contact with him. These words were meant for him. I lifted the award. "This goes out to him, the man I love. Griffin, you always say it's only us. It's us against the world, and I always loved that."

I returned the award to the podium after that. I had to in order to tell him what I wanted to next.

I stepped away from the stand and placed both hands on my dress, framing my stomach.

I looked up, leaning into the mic. "But I'll love the three of us even more."

Sound amplified around me, reverberated quite literally off the auditorium walls, but from where, I couldn't have determined at all. My focus was held to the man who gave me everything, who gave *us* our everything.

Griffin's gaze took hold of me as well, his attention traveling across the vast space to me on stage. Nothing could break it, people shaking his shoulders and his hands, and though he did reciprocate, his gaze didn't leave me.

His lips parted, a flush painting his cheeks that could be witnessed even from a distance. The large screens around the stage only confirmed that as the cameras zoomed in on him.

From somewhere music played. An arm went around my shoulders, and my award was slid into my hands—the actress. She placed it there, squeezing me.

I blinked, and Griffin did, too, my time was up on stage. He watched from all angles as I traveled offstage with my attendants, and I asked if I could go back down the way I came. I needed to get to Griffin.

"We'll have someone take you back to your seat from backstage, Mrs. Chandler," someone said to me, and "Congratulations on your new addition," came another. I was surrounded, and I barely got a chance to catch one more sight of Griffin. He had his hand on the seat in front of himself, craning his neck to see where they were taking me. I lost him behind the curtain.

"Um," I said, trying to fight my way out of the mass of people. Soon after I received one last hug from the woman who presented the statue to me, I politely escaped, trying to get back to the velvet barrier between my husband and me.

A male attendant touched my arm. "Mrs. Chandler, are you ready to go—"

"Just one second." I held up my finger but didn't make it to the curtain.

Backstage, screens had been set up to see the auditorium and a zoom over the crowd displayed a calming audience. The people had gotten themselves together, went quiet, nearly, and when the cameras passed over my seat, my seat next to Griffin's, I noticed two vacant chairs. Only Kerry and Kendrick sat in theirs, and a blast of anxiety shot through within me.

Where is he?

The attendant held out his arm that time. "I can take you back to your seat, Mrs. Chandler. If you're ready?"

But I wasn't ready. I...

"Roxie?"

His hand touched the small of my back, covering it, and his fingers twisted in the material of my dress, gesturing me to turn around.

I did, the attendant taking the award from me for a second, so helpful when he noticed me fumbling. Or maybe he just knew I needed my hands, that Griffin needed my hands.

He took them, his face really so flushed and eyes like a wave of crashing blue. He used to be so calm, but not anymore. It's clear by the way his nostrils were flaring. He was also out of breath, his broad chest rising and falling with his exerted breath.

He gripped my hands, running his thumbs over the tops of my wrists. That's how long his fingers were.

"Is it true?" he whispered, his gaze never leaving me, and I nodded, the tears stinging my eyes. I didn't know why I was fighting tears. Perhaps the hormones were already starting to have their way.

And then he did something stupid to me—he made the tears fall from my eyes. He made them fall by raising my hands, kissing the backs of them like they were the most beautiful thing he ever held, and I cried. I cried so hard.

A sheen misted his aqua blue eyes while he did. He kissed my hands again, blinking. "I'm going to be a dad?"

The tears touched the tops of my breasts when I nodded again. I was going to ruin my pretty dress, and I knew that when he touched my cheek. His other hand went to my belly, touching lightly, delicately, though I knew him to be so much stronger.

He put gentle pressure on my back, closing the space between us, and dipped to my level, touching our foreheads together.

"Thank you," he said, and I laughed. He did as well, chuckling as he shook his head. "I mean, I love you. I love you and me."

He placed both of his hands on my stomach, feeling him and me. I loved us both, too.

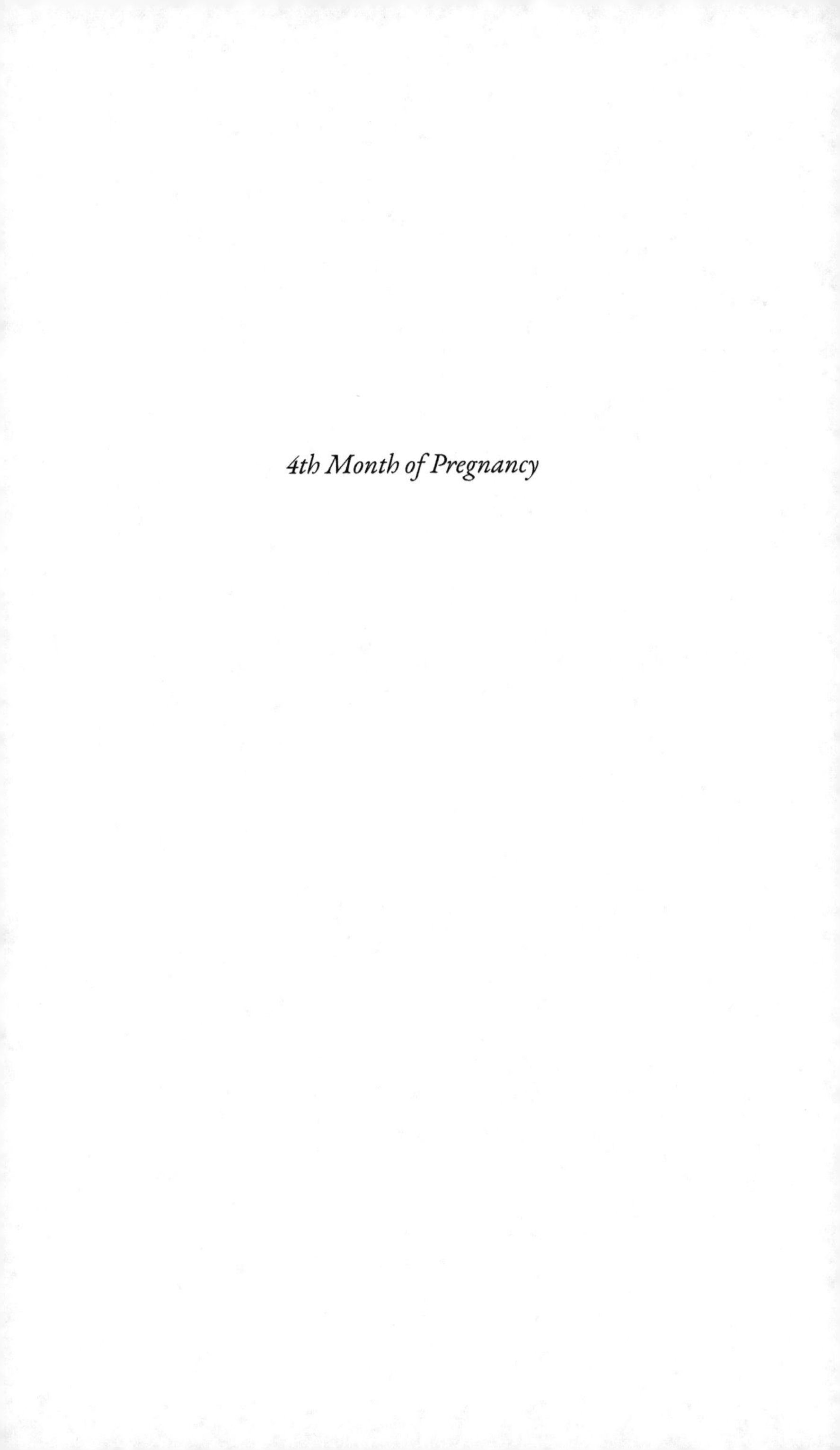

4th Month of Pregnancy

Two

GRIFFIN

I'D HEARD a lot of beautiful sounds in my life. The winning buzzer following an intense game on the court. The sound of my wife when I made her laugh, made her come... They were just a few of many I found myself fortunate enough to receive.

And then I got this.

The audible *thump, thump, thump* played subtly through the room like it wasn't the most wonderful sound in the world. I had heard it before, so many times but each listen always felt like hearing it for the first time. It flowed *through me* like the first time. Somewhere in a far off place, someone told me everything was okay. The heartbeat was fine, but they were wrong, the medical professionals. The heartbeat wasn't just fine. It was perfect, damn perfect, in every way.

A hand squeezing mine showed my wife's preparation for something we hadn't experienced before, and I leaned in, pressing a kiss to my Roxie's mouth.

"You ready for this?" I asked her sucking a bit on her plump lips. They were always so succulent.

Roxie's hand came into my hair, her mouth smiling while her big 'ole glasses smashed between us. She looked so cute in those things. A nod of her chin, and then we both faced the sonogram screen, waiting and breathing together.

"See that there?" the technician asked, smiling at us. She moved the little ultrasound stick around on Roxie's swollen belly as her other hand pointed to the screen that held my world—Roxie's and mine. A little nose showed with a small mouth underneath it. Little balled up fists covered the eyes directly above—always covering the eyes. The tech brought our attention to a certain area on the screen—her lips forming words, but I didn't hear anything after what she said next.

"A boy," she said.

A boy.

Jackson.

Roxie said the word at the same time my thoughts had even comprehended it all. Those large eyes of hers coated in unshed tears, making them a shiny shade of aquamarine green.

"Jackson," she repeated, and I nodded at her, confirming the name we'd picked out for a boy. Her tears started to fall and I kissed them away when she removed her glasses to wipe them.

"Yeah, Jackson," I told her, finding her cheek, her ear next. "Our Jackson."

About thirty minutes or so later, we were left alone after the tech, and later, the doctor came and went. We'd been given the okay once again—a good exam and healthy baby.

I helped Roxie dress, admiring her body. Her breasts were so swollen, her whole body flushed and filled with warmth. Her dark nipples erect, I couldn't help touching them, my fingers brushing the hard peaks before covering them with her bra. They were such a shame to cover up.

I went to clasp the bra behind her, but the resistance grew to be too much. I tugged her to me by the straps, kissing her shoulder as I fastened the clasps. She gasped as she placed her hands on her belly, her body shaking beneath my hands and so sensitive to my touch these days. Her chin tilted up, and I brushed a kiss against her cheek, admiring her rich, dark skin, and the ultra glow of her flesh. God, she'd never been more beautiful or sexier.

"God, Griffin..." she sighed, and I knew what that meant.

Forcing myself to stop, I pulled her dress up, painfully hard in my jeans. I slid the straps over her shoulders, and she laughed a bit upon rocking her plump little bottom back into me. She knew why I had to stop, too. I'd have her right back up on that exam table only too quickly. We had a few close calls before.

She had our pictures in her hand when we made it outside moments later, and that was okay by me because I got her other hand.

I gripped it, watching her while she lifted our baby's images into the Miami sun. Getting a little ahead of me, I noticed the bell of her dress swung across her shapely legs. It took all I had to get her to wear it today, my favorite dress on her, but it was hers, too, and I knew it made her feel pretty.

I kissed her hand. "You wanna tell everyone today?" I asked, referring to our news. I'd also known she'd have an opportunity to do so this afternoon—at least to a few of our close friends. Though, she didn't know that.

Shaking her head, she surprised me. "We should do something special," she said.

She yelped a little with glee when I spun her around, bringing her to me. We'd made it to my Range Rover at this point, and I leaned back on it, taking her with me when I brought her back into my arms.

"Oh, yeah?" I asked her, kissing the shell of her ear. She pushed all her hair up above her head that day. Between that and her glasses, she looked like an adorable little nerd and I squeezed, pushing a giggle out of her.

I warmed her neck with my mouth. "What did you have in mind?"

"There was this couple I saw online," she said, her lids closing over her eyes. "They did this thing with chalkboards and wrote the sex and the baby name on it and—"

"I wanna do it." I left her neck to shift her body and see her. I tipped her chin. "Whatever it is, I want to do it."

Her hands came down flat on my chest, moving up to go around shoulders. "But will you have time? To do a photo shoot? I know, you've already been stretching yourself thin with all these appointments for the baby and stuff."

Yeah, but God knew I could stand to do more. I'd been pretty present, but unfortunately, the unpredictability of my training and event schedule had left her to her own devices during enough of these appointments to know I wasn't being stretched thin as much as I should be.

I rocked her by the hips. "I'll let Deanna know. She'll handle it. She'll schedule the shoot and make sure I'm there," and she knew my agent would. The woman was a tank and handled anything I threw at her and had since Roxie found her for me. I was technically Roxie's first client, with her before the official business of her consulting firm broke ground. She'd found Deanna for me through research and hard work, which made me one of the many players Roxie made sure ended up with good people around them. Since Deanna came into my life, I had no problems, and my woman made that happen for me.

That settled, I took Roxie around the silver SUV. A few paps lingered across the street, on standby to capture whoever they could and the shutters snapped our way.

I waved, acknowledging them before helping my wife into the car, and after I had, she did the craziest thing. She actually rolled the window down, waving back to them, and I could kiss her for it. In fact, I did after we took off and halted at a stoplight. Coming to Miami, living in the limelight had been weird for us both at first, but together we got through it.

"I think I want snicker doodles," she hummed, gripping her belly at the thought. She turned her head on the seat. "The bad ones with sugar and frosting and terribleness. Can we stop at a bakery on the way home?"

Chuckling, I smoothed my hand down hers, kissing it before checking my watch. I guess we had a little time.

She had her snicker doodles by the time we pulled up to the house, the driveway lined with the pink flowers she planted just last summer. I told her we could get a landscaper, but she wanted to do it all on her own, knee deep in the dirt.

So I got down there with her.

We'd filled the boxes outside the windows with them, as well, the terra cotta roof of the white-walled home I built for us once upon a time complimented by them. Our running fountain surrounded by a circle driveway led up to the whole shebang, and that driveway was filled. In fact, completely to the brim.

Vehicles of many different makes and models filled the driveway, some flashy and some not. The orange Bugatti, I had a feeling, was one of my guests. My friends tended to show off when they knew other folks would be around. My boys and I would stay out of Roxie's way, though. I'd just be there for support.

"What's going on?" Roxie was licking her fingers at that point, sugar all around her pink tinted lips, and I laughed, taking the cookie box from her.

"Baby, let me help you," I said, taking one of the napkins the bakery gave us to her face. She'd never let me live it down if I let her go in there all sugary.

Her hands came up to mine, fighting me a little.

"What? I…"

I got her wrists. "Relax. Your only job is to look pretty, which you do, so we're good. Just be easy."

"Be easy? Pretty?" Alarm hit her eyes, making them flare in their jade color. "What are you talking about? What did you do?"

I popped a kiss on her nose. "You got your last question five of them ago. So come with me, and just, well, have fun."

I wasn't going to lie. The questions ensued, but I held to my guns, being more than evasive as I managed to get her to allow me to hide the cookie box. We left it in the car and headed up the walk, the oak doors opening seemly by themselves for us.

The entire home was open when we got inside, the curtains drawn and light bouncing throughout the foyer. In that foyer stood people and I had to say, each and every one of them put a surprise in my wife's eyes.

I had a bit of that surprise, too, at who'd been able to make it out, but not really. Even with our friends' busy schedules, they dropped everything to be here today, support Roxie and our baby. I invited some of our closest friends in Miami, a small baby shower of what I knew would be many for Roxie down the road. Hell, she'd already had two, one thrown by her co-workers at her consulting firm and even my family had already thrown one for her, as they all just couldn't wait. Roxie's close friends had shown up to that last one, too, everyone excited.

Today's event was to see our Miami friends, the connections we'd developed over the years since coming here. Some of my fellow players, their wives, and many others who'd found their way into Roxie's and my life turned up. We'd gained a lot of support since coming here, a lot of love, and each one of them had something that had my wife put her hand to her chest.

We were surrounded by colorful balloons, gifts, and all kinds of stuff, and at the root, it was all there for Roxie. I had a gift myself in the crowd, too, something special I thought she'd really like. I couldn't give that woman enough, but well, I thought I'd try.

A collective "surprise!" hit the air, and the cute, little pregnant woman in the room jaw dropped. Her hand came up to her cheek, and almost instantly, her lashes flashed when her pinkie touched her eyeglasses arm.

She ripped her glasses off, pulling her hair down next.

"Griffin," she edged out through her teeth, shoving her glasses behind her. "Why didn't you say something? I could have done something with my hair. I..."

After taking her glasses for her, I grabbed her by the hips.

"You're not in sweats, babe," I whispered in her ear, knowing I had at least succeeded in that. "And you look beautiful. You always look beautiful."

A smashed kiss on her face elicited an "aww" from the group, as well as a few taunts from who I knew to be my buddies in the group. I'd deal with them later, but right then, I had to show my wife to her first of many surprises. She went willingly, her hand in mine, and outside our French doors, could only be described as crazy. I knew because I approved it all prior to the party.

She had the whole set up, my girl. Pretty music and food for days. Roxie had a thing for owls, and they decorated nearly every piece of edible art, and that's exactly what it all was, from her cake to her cookies. The theme of purple, gray, and blue splashed throughout. Her favorite colors. Even the punch was decked out in an ice sculpture design, and to the right of it, a guy sat oh so casually in an arrangement of folding chairs placed for the soon-to-be mom and her guests to open gifts.

Troy stood, tugging down his blazer, and if Roxie wasn't in tears by the set up already, she was then. She cried quite frequently these days at things she found emotional, or beautiful, or really anything at all.

Weeping, Roxie left my hands and went to the man who'd made our day so special once before.

Our old wedding planner hugged her, the little bump outlined between them making him laugh. Sliding from her hands, he held her out, admiring her.

"My bride— Oops!" he paused, covering his mouth. "I guess I should say my mom-to-be. You look gorgeous, sweetheart. So gorgeous."

The compliment caused her head to lower, shy. She shook her head. "What are you doing here?"

"Well, I've been recruited," he said, raising her hands to our terrace. The beach was rolling in the background—the setup made quite the scene.

He lowered her hands. "As well as a special project."

His gaze found mine as he handed her off to me. That would be the last time I intervened before I let her enjoy her party, have her moment. She deserved it all.

I brought her to me. "Troy's going to design the baby's room, and he's ready to get started whenever you are ready."

It was something she hadn't had time to get to since my wife was so busy at her firm. We had the space set aside right next to ours, but the room was a canvas at this point, and I figured with Troy, she could make it her own.

The waterworks began after my announcement—my special gift to her, and I let her go for it. I knew they were nothing but happy tears.

～

Roxie

How did he always manage to do things like that, surprise me in ways that bordered on extraordinary?

The gifts open and farewell wishes bestowed upon me from just a few of the best people in my life, all I could think about was who was responsible for all the day's joy. I'd been showered with so much love and a multitude of congratulations, as well as, warm regards, and I did nothing particularly special at all to even receive it. It had just been given to me, blessed to me by the best man and soon-to-be father that ever existed.

I found him in the kitchen that night after my guests had left, doing of all things he could do—dishes. Bent over the sink, Griffin had soap up to his elbows, scrubbing away at the dishes inside.

Hitching my hip against the kitchen's archway, I just looked at him for a moment, his t-shirt stretched over his back and pulled taut over his biceps. His feet bare, Griffin's distressed jeans covered the tops. I went over to him, sliding my hands into the back pockets of his jeans.

I hugged him, as I squeezed that perfect round curve covered by denim.

"Have I told you that you're like kinda perfect," I told him, rubbing my forehead into his back. His scent I could bathe in.

He dashed me a smile over his back, sliding until he turned the tables on me and had my bottom pressed up against him. How was he always able to do that? Using a rag, he dried himself off, then encased his long arms around my waist.

"The last hour I'm drawing a blank on," he said, smoothing his hands down my hips. "Maybe you should tell me again and boost my ego a little more."

He got an elbow jab for that one, a fake one, but still. He fought me on it though, a chuckle in his voice as he grabbed my elbow. Dipping down, he pressed his mouth to my neck, his teeth skidding the skin, and something hot struck through me, my entire body flush with heat.

I breathed, closing my eyes, and suddenly my hand was taken. I opened my eyes.

"What are you doing?" I asked him, a giggle in my voice. He was taking me away, out of the kitchen and down the hallway.

His finger went up to his lips. "A surprise."

I didn't think I could take any more surprises. He'd been so wonderful, but I kept silent, playing his game. Soon enough, we ended the tour in our bedroom. I had a feeling what his surprise was, but then he left me there, standing square on our Aztec rug. He'd actually hired a decorator for the room, and over the years we both added our personal touches. The rug had been Griffin's idea.

I grabbed the bedpost, sitting down. I actually more so ended up falling down. I was still getting used to the weight I gained from the baby thus far, and I plopped, falling to my back a little.

Griffin saw me the minute I let go of the post.

He rushed to bed.

"Baby!"

Reaching, he got the underside of my arm, and I waved him away, feeling silly.

"I'm fine," I said laughing a little. "Just a little embarrassed."

He had my waist then, getting me secure.

"Don't be," he said, holding me there. "You okay?"

"Mmmhmm. I swear. Just getting used to my new body."

Rubbing my tummy a little, I laughed and got that worry to leave Griffin's face as well, his handsome smile back. My feet aching from standing so long, I tried to rub them, but he took over, pushing the pad of his thumb into my instep and heaven came in the form of his fingers.

I moaned. "You're going to make me fall back again."

He grinned. "Is that a promise? I like you on your back."

He got toes into his side for that one, and that's when I noticed what was on the bed, a tiny package adorned with curly string. I reached for it, the package so small.

"What is this, Griffin?"

His broad shoulders shrugged. Putting his arm behind me, he got closer, surrounding me with him. "Maybe you should open it."

I eyed him. I didn't think I could survive another one of his surprises, but curiosity made me tug at the curly ribbon on the top.

"It's a gift for the baby," he said when I got part way through the ribbon. "My gift to Jackson."

Hearing him say his name made all of it feel so real. I kissed his cheek, popping the top open, and he helped me, reaching inside the box.

"Hold out your hands," he said, and I did, watching as he placed the tiniest pair of sneakers I'd ever seen. They had a side swoop and everything, black with matching lacing.

Out of his pocket, he pulled a little basketball, and saying that was the most adorable gift I'd gotten so far was an understatement.

But I had to have a little fun.

"Optimistic, huh?" I asked, fingering the tiny laces. I lay back on the bed, and he joined me, placing an arm around my waist.

He shrugged. "It's not optimistic. It's destiny. Our boy is destined, and I'm going to be there to make it happen every step of the way."

Taking the tiny shoes, he made the soles walk across my stomach, a handsome grin on his lips.

He looked at me. "I'm going to be there for him, Roxie.

And not just for basketball. I'll support him in whatever he wants to do, basketball or otherwise."

Why was I not surprised? I should never be when it came to my husband.

"I like the sound of that," I said, incredibly warm inside. He had a way of doing that.

Almost like a summons, a tickle in my tummy had my hand moving to my stomach, and as Griffin recognized the gesture, he placed his hand there also. He hadn't felt movement yet because the initial flutters deep inside were too small for him to feel anything, but that never stopped him. I think he wanted to feel connected, to me, the baby, and Lord knows how much I adored him for that.

Together, we held hands, mine feeling for the general area of that second tickle. It hit, and at my reaction, Griffin smiled.

Drawing in, he leaned over me, kissing my tummy with his eyes closed.

I gripped his head, blond tendrils flowing through my fingers. I felt the connection, as well. I felt it everywhere, especially when his hand moved to my dress.

He pushed underneath the material, palming my hip, my ass, and using the flesh, he brought me to him, my belly between us until he turned me to my side.

He got above me, his hand reaching behind his back. He gathered his shirt, tugging it off, and golden skin, rugged with tiny hairs made its appearance. His body spaced off into perfect sections, his skin stretching over hard flesh with every move he made toward me.

I wanted to touch him, his hair messy and tossed from removing his shirt, but it turned out he wanted to touch me more.

"Griffin..."

His hand gripping my ass summoned me to turn.

"On your knees," he said, his voice laced with something carnal, his drawl rough.

I did as I was told, a noise escaping my throat as his hands massaged my hips. He reached for the zipper of my dress and my head sagged forward, the gentle undoing of the metal fastener heated to my sensitive skin.

It seemed he had a free hand because suddenly my folds were pinched through my panties, his thick fingers rough against my throbbing lips.

I called out when he slid inside against my aching bud, kissing my neck, then my shoulder when he moved my dress and bra strap down my arm. I ached for him, my panties slick and saturated and suddenly, Griffin lowered them, tonguing the vertebrae of my spine while he drew them down.

On my knees, I maneuvered out of them, and Griffin unstrapped my bra, letting it and my dress straps fall to my wrists.

My heavy breasts spilled forward at the relief, and I used the bedding in an attempt to relieve the ache around my distended nipples as they skid against the sheets.

He had me so vulnerable that way, so exposed, and his hands came to spread my cheeks, pushing my bottom up.

"So sweet," he said, breathing over my heat. "You smell so damn sweet, Roxie. So fucking sweet."

And he tongued me, immersing himself so deep when he penetrated. My arms weakened at the depth and my body racked in shudders. As if he knew, he supported my hips, holding me while his mouth sucked, summoning more juices.

I fell to my elbows, burying my face in my pillows. I called his name, his hands bringing my hips to his face, my core to his mouth. The pressure ripped through me, his hand reaching up to palm my breast. I was diamond-hard under his touch.

"Come, baby," he breathed from behind. "Come for me."

I was so close.

Fighting it, I reached behind me, tugging his arm so he'd get on top of me. He did, getting up on his knees, and I turned unbuckling his pants.

He drew in close from behind, letting me push his pants down.

His lips were completely swollen, hot pink and covered with my taste.

Jeans down to his hips, his length descended, arching up to the first section of his abs.

Using the thick flesh, he drew it between my cheeks, sliding his hand down my back. He laid me on my side, then got behind me as the hard ridges of his body embraced me, protecting me from everything.

Lifting my leg, he stretched me, a breath escaping his lips into my ear.

"Let me fill you, Roxie," he said, kissing the shell. "Open up for me."

I closed my eyes, feeling him all around and deep at the same time. So long, he tore me apart from the inside out, and he rocked, fluttering his hips to gain even more depth.

He fingered my breasts, tweaking my nipples, and I couldn't breathe, the pressure inside building toward the brim. We were so close, as close as we could ever be, his thighs slapping the back of mine.

Drawing my hair back, he pushed his lips against the nape of my neck, his hips moving in quick time, as he took me to the brink. He whispered his love to me with every thrust, his body rock, and his kiss hard.

"I love you, too," I told him, but the words didn't feel like enough. They never did no matter how many times I said them. My love for this man ran deep. There were no words for it that were completely good enough.

Warm jets only came after my own heat flourished from me, the combination dripping hot down my thighs. He came so hard with me, the length of his arm reaching around to take me with him.

"You'll always have me," he soothed, brushing his lips across my back. He moved his hips again, milking me and exhausting us both.

"That's my promise to you both," he said, and I could feel that, the emotion deep in his voice. His love for me, *us,* ran just as deep. I bet if someone asked him he'd say even more.

I know because I would, too.

Three

ROXIE

I CURLED my leg over my lengthy bed pillow, a constant roll in the form of the house doorbell drumming around in my head.

Groaning, I hugged the second love of my life, trying to ignore the sound but decided I knew better. It could be important. I sighed, falling to my back and my hand hit a piece of paper. It crumbled a bit in my fingers as I brought it up to my face, and squinting, I made out the fine cursive. He always did write better than me.

"Hey, I wanted to wake you, but knew better of it as you had Samson between your thighs."

I snickered. Griffin knew the pillow. He *got* the pillow, the thing a staple in my pregnancy so far, and was actually quite cool about the other man in my life. I smiled.

· · ·

"Anyway, I got a long one today, as I'm sure you know since you have my schedule. I'll check in when I can. I love you. Give Jackson a squeeze for me. I gave him a kiss already. - Griff."

That thing he did to me I couldn't put into words. It was a good thing he was so well-versed with them.

The drum around the house continued, and I whined, making myself get up to get it. I had a routine in the morning that usually consisted of Samson and the bedpost.

I got him, using the post to get to the edge of the bed. My slippers were down on the rug, and I slipped inside them, finding a nightgown I had lying around.

I was still naked from last night. Grinning, I got myself together, then found a robe, which made me completely decent. I shimmied out of the bedroom and down the hall after that, anticipating a salesman or something at the door. Because of that, I got my lines all ready, but nothing could prepare me for the man behind the door.

In a snazzy blazer, Troy beamed at me, always sunshiney at what barely could be eight in the morning. He had two men behind him, wearing jeans and construction boots. One had a pencil behind his ear, and I couldn't have been more confused.

My old wedding planner and friend gathered me into his arms.

"Morning, sweetheart. Simply gorgeous at any hour," he said, pulling away. He held my hands, swinging them a little and I laughed.

"Uh, thanks." I had to say I loved the flattery, but it was kind of hella early. I scratched the back of my head, and I think it dawned on him that I had no idea why he was there.

His head tilted. "Mommy-to-be, you've already forgotten? Eight o' clock consultation? You said you wanted to get started right away with the baby's room."

Crap. We had discussed that. With all the excitement yesterday, I must have let that slip my mind. I was completely drunk on punch and sugar yesterday.

I covered my mouth, my fingers falling away. "Oh, Troy, I'm sorry. We did agree to that."

My brain lapse caused him to chuckle. He grabbed my hand. "It's not a problem. We can reschedule."

But he'd come all that way, *twice* at that, and I knew what people had to go through to get here. That ferry ride wasn't a joke.

Griffin and I lived off Miami's coast, the only way to get into the city by ferry.

I waved my friend off, gesturing him inside next. "We can do it today. No problem. My morning is completely free." That was why I gave the "okay" so quickly. Plus, I wanted to see my friend again. We didn't talk as much since he moved to New York. Troy had businesses all over the country but chose to put his central office there, selling everything from planning services to merchandise with his name on it, a true entrepreneur I could only admire. He'd even had a hand in decorating my consulting office, *Rox Inc.*

Troy, of course, protested about today. Especially, after he learned I had been sleeping, but I insisted, more than excited to get started on the baby's room. The place had essentially turned into a black hole of "we should do this to it," and because of that, there were random swatches of fabrics and paint samples everywhere. It also had become a dumping ground for everything we'd gotten for the baby so far.

Troy, the dear he was, tried not to look surprised at the monstrosity of strollers and toys, but an "Oh, my" did fall from his lips at first glance. He recovered quickly though, telling his team to measure while he sat with me in the breakfast nook. He spread out notebooks and samples on the counter while I made him coffee. He liked two sugars and cream.

"Thank you," he said, tipping his cup to me after I'd made it and I smiled, my hand on my chin from my seat at my counter next to him. Eventually, a small snicker came from my right, and I dropped my hand, eyeing him.

"What?" I asked, feeling more than confused.

He waved his fingers. "Nothing. Now, let's go over—"

"Uh-uh." That man would not laugh at me and *not* let me in on it. I crossed my arms. "Spill it."

He grinned, pointing ahead. "You were staring at that wall for more than a minute, the biggest smile on your face. I called your name twice, and you said nothing."

Had he? I really did have pregnancy brain. I pressed my hands to my cheeks. "I'm sorry."

"It's fine," he said, placing his cup down. "You're just happy. That, and you look rather satisfied this morning."

"Troy!" I pushed his arm, and that sent his head back in laughter.

He raised his hands. "You asked. And where is the husband? No doubt trying to find the perfect star for you? He spared no expense for the party yesterday, Roxie, and the baby is meant to have the best that can be had. I offered the services for both at no cost. My present to you both, but he wouldn't have that. Eventually, I gave in. He was a man with his mind made up and wouldn't be swayed."

Nothing he said surprised me. Griffin and his heart were so big. He always wanted the best for me. He'd always taken care of me.

The doorbell rang again, and I squeezed Troy's hand before getting up. He said he'd get everything set up for us to begin and I told him fine while I answered the door. I checked the peephole before opening, but that time, I didn't know the visitor.

A woman, older with short gray hair, held a large bag, smiling up at me. She held out her hand. "Mrs. Chandler?"

I let go of the door, accepting her hand. "Yes, can I help you?"

A shake of her head, read of her confusion. "I'm here for the interview."

And then, I was the one confused. I leaned against the door. "I'm sorry? Interview?"

Her head bobbed once in acknowledgment. "For the nanny position."

My eyes widened, and I watched as she pulled a form out of her bag. On the paper, read her name: *Pamela Harris.* Down below read a resume with quite a few high profile clients. There were people I saw on the silver screen and ranking the music charts, but my mind was still blown why she was here. I never sent out for a nanny at all. I mean, the baby wasn't even born yet.

I held my stomach, feeling weird about it all.

"Are you all right, Mrs. Chandler?"

"Um, yes," I said, blinking. "I'm sorry. Who contacted you again?"

"It was a woman by the name of Deanna Bloom. She said she represented your husband."

Relief came a bit at the name of Griffin's agent. At least, I wasn't losing my mind. But still, I hadn't given her permission to do that. I wanted to get to the bottom of this it all, but didn't want to leave the woman standing outside.

I waved her. "Please, uh. Come inside."

She nodded, following me. In the foyer, I told her one moment while I made a call. I found my cell phone on the nook counter, and Troy's head lifted.

"Everything, okay, Roxie?"

Dialing, I pressed the phone to my ear. "Yeah, just have to make a quick phone call."

I took it down the hall, staring out the window toward the beach. I really loved living there, the place so open. The waves were the first thing I saw in the morning, and the voice of the man who made that happen sounded in my ear.

"Morning, baby."

He had the power to elicit this light in me, something beyond even my control.

I turned toward the glass sliding door, resting my head on it. "Hi. What are you doing?"

"Another damn tedious day," he said, breathing into the phone. "I've already had two meetings this morning. I had to get them in before practice this afternoon."

"Meetings?"

"Yeah, just more endorsement stuff. You know, the usual."

Very high in demand my guy. He learned to balance all that, though, and his agent had been great to help him with that. Nothing like his first disaster with Mickey and his first publicist Rich thank God.

"Anyway, how's my girl?" he went on. "Everything, okay? The baby?"

I touched my stomach. "We're all cool. Good and everything, but I wondered if you could call Deanna for me about something."

"Sure. What do you need?"

I breathed into the phone, pushing off the glass. "There's a woman here. A nanny? She said Deanna scheduled her for an interview with me. I appreciate it and everything, but I don't have a need for—"

"Oh, that was me, Roxie."

"You?" I blinked, shaking my head. "What was you?"

"I made some calls this morning. Got Deanna to set up some meetings with you for some help."

"But..." I didn't want to say it, but why would he do that? Instead, I went with this. "Um, uh... But why?"

The phone held a steady silence for a moment, but then came his deep voice.

"Well, we kinda talked about it a little, babe."

We had I guess, but so, so briefly. It had been a fleeting conversation over a few dinners, but nothing we settled on. I heard of those stories, celebrity nannies raising the kids instead of the parents and that unsettled me. I wanted to form those connections with my child. I wanted us both to.

"Yeah, I guess, but…" I paused, drawing my lip between my teeth. "We didn't come to a firm decision on that."

"No, but we need the help, Roxie. Don't you think? What about when you go back to work full-time?"

I breathed.

"Just consider it. Talk to a few of these women scheduled for today. They come highly recommended, and it would really set my mind at ease that we have a plan. And that's all this is—a plan. I don't want you worrying about anything right now. Just being cute and pregnant and sexy as hell."

My cheeks ablaze, I put my hand to one. He always made sure to remind me of that, how he saw me in his eyes.

"Please?" he questioned, sounding all cute himself. I could also hear that lip pouting through the phone.

"You always get your way."

"Well, I'll take this one. I love you and have fun today. It's for you."

Four

GRIFFIN

THE WEEKEND FOUND me on the golf course, but the rounds weren't much for leisurely activity. I had my cell phone in my hand more than my nine-iron, and my inviting party was starting to notice. I gazed up, my agent, one of my team's owners, and his friend's eyes all on me.

My smile went crooked.

"Sorry," I said putting my phone away. I rested my hands on the club. "My wife is pregnant, so every buzz in my pocket is like a straight twinge of paranoia from if she's okay to do I need to pick up something for her."

Shit, I even imagined the buzz when it *wasn't* buzzing these days. I couldn't help it I guess. The golf course had some distance between the house and me, and I got like this anytime I couldn't get to Roxie quickly. It's not like she needed me really. In fact, it was rare she ever really needed anything, but as she got further and further along in her pregnancy, *I* became more and more aware of whenever physical distance was put between us for my job. We'd learn to balance that over the years with just the two of us, but this was completely new territory, intimidating territory.

Deanna chuckled like I knew she would. The only woman on the course, she looked right at home with the boys. If fact, she could putt the pants off all of us—her age only making her more experienced. She'd agented in a male-dominated industry for over thirty years, so let's just say she played a lot of damn golf.

She put her putter on her shoulder, turning to our other two players. "Griffin is definitely a family man."

"That he is."

The words came from who'd grown to be a good friend to me over the years through me playing for him.

Greg Offerman was one of the more hands on team owners of Miami. We always saw him swing by our practices and he was one of the first benefactors to Roxie and my charity organization. He was quite active in it as well as he would speak at events when he could. I was grateful for everything he'd done for me and my brothers on the team, and like I said, he'd come to be a good friend, so I never liked to turn him down when he invited me out for a game. That day, he'd brought in some exec from Los Angeles, a good friend of his he'd said, and I didn't mind.

He squeezed the guy's shoulder, Roddy, I believe his name was, though he called him Rod sometimes.

Greg stared up at me. "That's why Griff is one of my best. He has his priorities straight. Family first and business second, and it's that balance that brings out the magic."

Rod swapped out a club for another from the caddy. "You're right, Greg. A very good quality." The choice seemed to please him because he passed a rather large bill into the boy's hand in response.

Upon setting the club to the green, he smiled at me. "The court, in general, could use more of that," he said, then nudged Greg. "Have I found your secret to a winning team?"

That sent us all laughing, Greg's hand coming down on

my shoulder. "Now, if I could only get his brother to sign with us for next season."

I got the look in his eye before he gave it to Deanna.

She lifted her hands, her graying black hair swaying under her visor. She was acting representation until my brother acquired someone on his own. Colton had just graduated college recently, and well, he had a reputation already back at Texas State—a good one and having a brother in the game already didn't hurt him either.

Deanna chuckled. "I've given him your proposal."

"Mmm, yes," Greg grunted, then pointed at me. "So now it's time to bring him around to the right side. He has no use for LA."

Not one to get in my brother's business, I waved my hands. "You know, I can't go there. My brother does what he wants to do."

He was more stubborn than all of us in that way, and I also knew him to have his heart set on LA. He wanted beaches, and yeah, woman as he was only twenty-two. Miami had both those things, but they also had me, and I knew well that *I* wouldn't want my older brother cock-blocking me. I also had quite a rep here myself, and he probably wanted to make something of his own. I could only respect that.

"Maybe one day," Greg concluded. He got his own club from the caddy, then led us on to the next hole, and that's when the phone made its appearance again.

I apologized the moment the buzzing made everyone laugh. I wondered if all guys got like that when their wife was pregnant. First timer, here.

"This or that?" the text said, and next it followed up with a picture of Roxie holding bibs. One had a little red car on it and another a basketball.

Shaking my head, I asked her if she was serious with that question.

Then, she sent me another message: *:P*

I laughed.

"Basketball it is then ;)" she texted.

A throat cleared and all eyes on me had me waving them off. Dang, couldn't a guy text his pregnant wife these days without getting a hard time?

I played the situation off, shrugging casually. "Nothing dire. She's just shopping."

Deanna's hand came down on my arm. "Oh, buddy. Make sure she never hears that."

Again, this guy over here was only getting a hard time.

The rest of the morning went a lot like the beginning, friendly conversation as we went from hole to hole, and I found I didn't have to analyze my phone as much. Roxie's texts had pretty much dwindled down to nothing, and I assumed she had gotten her shopping done for the time being. With them more sporadic, I settled into the game a bit more and enjoying time out got a little easier with every hole. I realized then I had been a little on edge recently. These were all just new experiences Roxie and I were having at home, so I guess I was still adjusting to them.

Once I really got into the game, my competitive nature came back, and I wasn't distracted anymore as I sunk hole after hole in a few strokes.

"Winner buys lunch," Greg said, nudging me. He placed his putter to the green. Tapping, he missed the hole by several good inches, cursing, before bringing the iron to his shoulder. "Like I said. Winner buys, and I find myself pretty hungry today, Griff."

So, this was how these people played, huh? I chuckled. "Sure thing, Greg. But if that's how we're playing I expect back lunches for previous games." He usually blasted Deanna and me out of the water. Today had been the exception to the rule.

His belly jutted when he laughed. "Touché."

After handing off his club to the caddy, he went over to Rod who'd been watching our exchange with a smile. Greg squeezed his shoulder. "The boy sure is something, isn't he? Smart as a whip and not afraid to tell it to this old goat."

He nudged his friend, chortling, and Rod nodded under his visor. The two stepped off heading towards the location of Rod's ball on the green and Deanna and I followed. After a few steps, I noticed hers were a bit slower than the party we were with.

"You know what this is, right?" she asked during our walk, and I shook my head. Her chin tipped toward the others only paces away. "He's chatting you up, Griffin. You know Roddy is scouting for his next picture?"

That had me stopping a little, setting my club to the green. This seemed casual enough as the two ahead had stopped as well. Roddy set his club down, aiming it, and I faced Deanna.

"Picture?" I asked speaking from the side of my mouth. Greg had mentioned Roddy came from LA but failed to mention the specifics of what he did for a living.

Deanna nodded. "He's got ins at Paramount. Word on the street is he's looking for an athlete for a cameo in his studio's next production." She paused a sec to watch him putt, squinting into the sun. "Sounds like your name is being put in."

Talk about all new territory. Film was something I'd *never* done before. My experience with acting had been mostly commercial with a few television appearances over the years. And those had been reality shows; things I'd accidentally been a part of as my friends were stars of some of their own. I'd gotten a few offers for some myself. Especially after all that happened in my first year.

Roxie and I had a rough one when we originally moved here. Her history of web videos she'd done in college had quickly been dug up. Things from her past were exposed to the world by greedy people *I'd* brought into our lives. Naturally, after the scandal hit the media, people wanted to see more of us. They wanted us to tell our *own* story. But in the end, we decided to decline. We knew our story, so what did it matter what anyone else thought?

This thing with Roddy would be different, though. And who knew, it could offer opportunities to a new world in my career.

Deanna patted my back, most likely thinking the same. The fellas seemed to be ready to move on. They geared up, heading toward their golf cart. Deanna and I went to ours, then we both waited for the two to take off as they were ahead of us.

Buzz.

I couldn't help but smile, pulling my phone out of my pocket. The texts from Roxie began again, and I answered letting her know what I was up to when she asked how I was.

"The day is nice," I told her. *"Just trying to relax a little."*

"You deserve it," she responded, and I loved her for that. *"I won't bug you anymore. I just wanted to let you know I'll have my phone off for the next hour or so."*

That confused me a little. She never turned off her phone.

"What's up?" I asked.

"Nothing. Just seeing Dr. Dow."

I sat up, the world stopping.

Everything stopped.

Roxie saw her counselor still but not so much for care these days. They had occasional lunch outings, but as far as I knew, they hadn't had a counseling session in quite a well.

"Everything, um," I paused during the text, unsure of it. I never asked Roxie about her counseling sessions unless she wanted to share. Her relationship with her counselor was a

personal one, and I never violated that, but seeing as how she hadn't sought care in so long... and with her being pregnant...

"Everything, okay?" shot from my fingertips, and I hit send before I thought better of it.

"Yeah, fine. Going for a quick talk. I'll text you after I'm done. Love you. Have fun today."

Have fun today. Have fun...

"Hey, Griff?"

Greg had his hand at the top of his golf cart, grinning. "Looks like we're both off the hook. Roddy has offered to buy us all lunch," he said, nudging his friend. He brought an arm around him, shaking. "We'll pick a place downtown and make an afternoon of it. Sound good?"

Deanna glanced my way, and I didn't miss the slight nudging she herself gave me with her arm.

My phone burned in my hands, the screen long blank.

Going for a quick talk, she'd said, but in the back of my mind, I wondered...

But why?

Five

ROXIE

Dr. Dow placed her hands over her jeans, always so casual in her demeanor. I missed that. She tilted her head, a set of square black frames on the tip of the older black woman's nose.

"How have you been, Roxie?" she asked, no notebook today. It was just us today. "It's been a little while for us, hasn't it?"

"It has," I said literally feeling that time. Adjusting, I had to find the right position on the couch. I definitely hadn't been pregnant the last time I had a session. It had been that long.

I placed my hands over my purse in my lap. "I'm sorry about that."

She lifted her hand from her knee, waving me off. "That wasn't a reprimand."

That I knew, but still, I did feel bad. I used to meet with her all the time, and now, we only met casually. Luncheons and what have you in a less formal setting, but sitting here in the present it seemed as if we hadn't missed a beat, her downtown office always welcoming.

"How's Griffin?" she asked. "The baby?"

Those were two topics that I could never grow bored discussing, my thoughts only happy to linger on them both.

I smiled. "Good. Griffin's great, and the baby," I said, placing my hand on him. I felt him immediately, that flutter. He must have had a spot he liked right on my left side. I liked to think of it as his little cubby hole.

I laughed a little. "He's getting big. Healthy."

"Mmm. *He*?"

Knowing I slipped, I sat back. "Yeah, we just found out the sex not too long ago. We're having a little boy. Jackson."

"That's a wonderful name, and I'm so happy for you both."

Everything with the baby still felt so surreal. I was happy, too. In fact, so much so that I felt I needed to see her that day, talk about things.

"So if we're good, did we just come to talk then?" she asked.

She got right to the point, Dr. Dow. She always knew how to do that.

Lacing my fingers over my stomach, I had no idea how to broach the subject. I didn't know what brought me here today. I just felt compelled to and almost anxious in the urgency.

I dampened my mouth. "Honestly, I don't know why I'm here. I just felt like I had to."

I'd been tossing and turning these last few weeks. Like I said, anxious for some reason. I had so many racing thoughts and just really needed to get them out I think.

Dr. Dow looked at me during my thoughts, smiling ever so gently.

She lifted her hand. "You know, you never need a specific reason to come and see me, Roxie. If you feel like you should be here, then you should. No need to look for reasons."

That had always been her policy. She was someone for me to talk to about any and everything whether it was nothing or something. Before, that had made sense when I had so many things overwhelming me. They'd been the things to bring me in here initially, and though I felt I still had a lot to work through, and probably always would, for the first time in my life, I felt I had a sense of peace. And things had been peaceful, so much so.

"Roxie?"

My lashes flickered up. Dr. Dow had her head tilted, her hands on her knee.

She crossed an ankle behind the other. "What's on your mind, dear?"

God, so many things, but I had no way to voice them. There were that many and organizing them seemed like such a task.

"I guess I'm overwhelmed really."

"Overwhelmed?"

Chewing my lip, I nodded, sitting back into the couch. Jackson fluttered within his little cubby hole, and I laughed a little, pressing into my side.

That made the doctor laugh, too.

I sat up. "Things have been just so overwhelming. The baby," I said, smiling as I held him. "And everything with Griffin."

"You said he's been well?"

"He has and so well, Doctor. He's found that balance. With me, his job, and the baby. He's getting so many opportunities in his career, as well and he's so happy. And as far as Jackson, he's so excited."

The moment I announced my pregnancy, it had been like a light had created in both of us, and Griffin? It shined so much within him. He wanted to be a father so badly and basically, breathed the role already. I was giving him something he truly wanted, and I had been so honored to do so.

"And then there's the house," I went on. "We've made renovations since Griffin had it built and they all went through so well."

"Your dream home," Dr. Dow said, smiling.

That brightness spread out on my face as well. I know it did. A strand of my hair fell over my eyes when I acknowledged what she said with a nod.

"It is a dream," I told her. "My life is a dream, my business."

"I heard about your award," she said, sitting back. "Things are working out for you all around."

I never thought the world would embrace my little idea like they did, but *Rox Inc.* soared with its success.

So many athletes had been matched with industry professionals through my agency, and one of the first things I'd decided to do with the blessing of that success was start the *Chandler Foundation*, Griffin's support and partnership in tow. We'd had so much help from our friends with it, rooting for it as much as they had us.

Thinking back on the success of the foundation and my own success, too, I never would have dreamed such wonder would have been possible.

Not long after Griffin and I were married, I decided to go to law school, specializing in business law. I hoped by doing so I'd come out on the other end and be able to help people in some way. Never in my life did I think my education would allow me to do what I had. Griffin had given me startup money to go for my dreams. *Rox Inc.* had very much been born because of him. He always believed in me, believed in my visions. That's probably why the success had come in the way it had, and so quickly, I think; I had so much support.

"They are," I said, answering Dr. Dow's former question.

Things had been working well for me and I breathed just thinking about it.

"The award show had been quite a day."

"I can imagine. And everyone has been supportive? Your friends and family, of your foundation and your business endeavors?"

"Yes, so much." I got emotional anytime I thought about it. Griffin's whole family had come down to see the place, my office when it first opened. And then there had been someone else.

"My, um..." I said swallowing hard. "My dad. He's been the biggest cheerleader. He came down when *Rox Inc.* opened."

That news pushed a dimple in the corner of the doctor's cheek. "Did he?"

"Yeah, he, uh..." It must be the hormones. I pushed a finger under my eye, catching some dampness. "He had my whole office decorated with flowers, and when he found out about the baby, he did this thing. He..."

Emotional, I took a moment. I needed one.

I smiled, through blurry eyes. "He air mailed a stroller down. He said my mom used it. He said he and my mom used it with me."

The room filled with something, something that made my throat feel tight—something that squeezed everything inside me so tight. I tried to breathe it out, but I couldn't, a ripping sound hitting the air. A white tissue was then placed in front of my eyes, and I accepted the Kleenex the doctor had presented to me.

"I'm so sorry," I told her, pushing the tears out of my eyes.

Her graying locks swayed over her cheeks as she shook her head. "Don't apologize, Roxie. These are good tears. Only good."

Sniffing, I gazed up at her, feeling so silly. I smiled a little, crumpling the tissue. "I guess I'm just so... I'm just so..."

"Happy," she said, finishing for me. Reaching over, she grabbed my hand, squeezing, and I did the same back.

I laughed a little. "Yeah, happy."

Her hand still in mine, she leaned forward. "You're happy. You're happy, and everything is good."

She was right, essentially. Everything was good. So why was I here then? Why had I come?

"And everything will continue to be," she said, picking up the tissue box. She presented it to me, the widest smile on her lips. "So don't be scared of it. Just let yourself have it."

Let myself have it...

What an interesting thought.

I found myself outside about a half hour later, the tears dried and my thoughts moving in a different direction, a better direction. They didn't feel so scattered now, all over the place. In fact...

I believed a center for them might be on the horizon.

I laughed at myself a little when I got to the parking lot, searching for my car.

Had that been the problem? That things had almost been *too* good? How curious...

Let yourself have it, she'd said. *Let yourself have it.*

I took a moment, letting those words resonate.

Let myself have it. I could do that.

My hand in my purse in a search for keys, I nearly dropped the whole bag when I looked up and noticed a figure by my car. It had been a tall figure, a vast one with long legs and broad shoulders. He also had these cheekbones. They were sharp, high and complimented his full lips so well. And then there was his eyes, not sky blue, no. They were nearly clear, like ice in a cool drink.

Griffin pushed off my Mini Cooper's tire with his shoe, his brown leather lace-ups complementing his twill pants and Polo shirt so well, making him handsome. He had his glasses on today, too, a set of black rectangular frames. I'd never get over golfing Griffin, clean cut and styled. He was starting to look more and more Dad-hot these days.

Dad-hot.

I grinned to myself. He would be a dad soon, wouldn't he?

His arm came out as I got to my car, got to him, and he closed the space before I could even get all the way there. His lips went to my neck, his wingspan engulfing me.

"What are you doing here?" I asked him, but then I forgot. He kissed right under my earlobe. He made me warm, his long fingers to my hip and pulling me closer.

"The guys and I got done early," he said, and air pulled through his nose, a heated breath pushing against my skin when he released it. His throat made a noise after he did, something like a groan as he had to be enjoying my scent.

I loved it, but I laughed at what he said. I pushed my shoulder into his side. "I'm sure Deanna loves being known as one of the guys."

He shrugged a little, chuckling to himself when he pulled back.

"She'd have it no other way," he said, releasing me just enough to hold my hand. "I thought I'd take you to lunch. That is unless you have other plans?"

If I had the option, my plans would always consist of him and nothing else.

I nodded, letting him take me toward his Range Rover. He said we could pick up my car later. Once in his, Griffin took my seatbelt, helping me with it. I could imagine because it usually took me three or four tries before I heard the click. The belly made it a little hard to see the buckle.

I caught his cheek on his pull back, thanking him with my lips pressed to that warm skin.

He grinned a little, taking a moment to buckle his own seatbelt before starting the car. His phone buzzed in his pocket when he did, and though he took it out after, he didn't check it before tossing it into the cup holder. He slid his hand in mine instead, getting the car in gear with our fingers laced together on the gear shift on the center console.

He took us on the road, and I instantly went to my happy place—our hands together and him by my side.

"Your visit with the doctor go all right?" he asked me, glancing my way before switching gears. I noticed his phone buzzed again, but again he ignored it, sliding me another look as he awaited my answer.

I nodded at what he said, feeling even more at peace. Things had gone well with the doctor. She told me to be happy. She essentially told me *not* to worry. I guess things had been going so well that when I realized I found myself in a place of ease, it had freaked me out a little. I never recalled things being that easy in my life. I always had something on my mind. I always over thought things. I always...

I just wouldn't do that anymore. I would enjoy my life. I would enjoy my ease and truly feel that happiness. I turned my head on the seat, smiling at my husband. I think I wanted to tell him about today, how much I really had grown. In the past, I hadn't, but not really for any particular reason. I just never really went into detail of my sessions with the doctor and Griffin never asked. He just supported me in whatever way I needed him to. He stood by me and had since I started seeing her after my eating disorder a few years ago.

And that's exactly what we'd determined it was, a disorder stimulated by my many years of avoidance. I used to avoid so much, my past.

I was happy I didn't have to do that anymore.

I squeezed Griffin's hand. "Yeah, we—"

His phone buzzed again, and sighing, he kissed the back of my hand, giving an apologetic smile before picking up the phone. We'd stop at a light, and he swiped his thumb across the screen.

"Who is it?" I asked, staring at the light. I'd tell him once it changed.

He ended up seeing the green himself and placed the phone down. He shook his head, taking off again.

"Nothing," he said, turning the wheel. He looked at me. "You were saying? The doctor?"

"Oh, yeah. Everything went well. Fine."

"Oh, um. So you didn't—" When he stopped mid-sentence, he bit his lip. He ended up raising his hand.

"Never mind," he said. "But it went well?"

"Uh, huh. No big."

And then that phone buzzed again. We both glanced down at it and I frowned. His phone never buzzed that much, and if it did, he usually answered whoever. But again, for some reason, he didn't. He simply asked me where I wanted to go for lunch. The question was interrupted by at least three more text messages, and by the time we pulled up to one of our favorite restaurants, or I should say mine as he'd chosen to take me to the French place that had tasty sandwiches I enjoyed, I picked up his phone, deciding he should answer whoever was trying to get his attention.

"The sooner you do, the sooner they'll leave you alone," I said with a laugh, but he didn't. In fact, he seemed to want to do anything but.

He took the phone from me with a smile, pocketing it.

"It's really nothing," he said, getting out of the car. He came around and opened my door. "It's just Deanna."

"Yeah?" I asked, taking his hand, as he helped me step out. "What does she want?"

He closed the door behind me. "Nothing really. She's just giving me a hard time about lunch."

We'd started walking at this point, but I stopped on the sidewalk. "What about lunch?"

He pulled me in. "Nothing. Let's just—"

"What about lunch, Griffin?"

Standing tall, he pushed his hand into his pocket. "Greg invited the pair of us out with his friend Roddy."

"Okay. So why didn't you go?"

His eyes lifted, but then he smiled. "I guess because I had another way I wanted to spend the time, which consisted of me, you, and our baby. Is that a crime?"

It wasn't a crime, but I didn't want him thinking he couldn't do things he wanted to do just because of me. And then that phone buzz again, and I shook my head as Griffin escorted us toward the bistro. The doors opened for us via the restaurant's attendants, and we both thanked them before heading toward concierge. Griffin actually ended up shutting off his phone by the time we were seated.

That's how bad Deanna was trying to get a hold of him.

"That sounds more than her giving you a hard time," I said picking up my menu. The way his phone was buzzing one would think something crazy was happening on her end. "And you can go out with your friends, you know?"

He nodded behind his own menu. "I know. But I don't want to handle any business today. You were out today. With the doctor and I…, I figured I'd spend the time with you—"

"Wait. What? Business? What business? I thought you said this was lunch with friends."

A breath escaped his lips. He put the menu down. "It is, but Greg's friend is also a movie producer. Deanna thinks Greg set the golf outing up because he wanted Roddy to meet me. I guess he's looking for an athlete for a cameo in his new film."

I nearly choked on the water I just sipped. Eyes wide, Griffin came around to my side of the table, patting me down.

"I'm fine," I said, laughing a little. And once he realized I was, his arm settled down behind me.

I pushed his side. "A film? Were you going to mention that?"

A deep chuckle rumbled from his chest. "I thought it was just Deanna being Deanna. But apparently, Greg really was doing that because they're talking about it now. That's what the texts are about. She's updating. Has since I left."

Reaching to my side, I got my purse, then maneuvered to get up. But as Griffin was on my exit side I couldn't move.

"What are you doing?" he asked.

I tilted my head, eyeing him. "You need to go to that lunch."

"Roxie." His hand came down on mine, lowering them both to my lap. "I told you. I'm eating lunch with you today. Deanna will handle it."

We could eat lunch together any day, though. Things like this, things as big as this didn't happen every day.

I looked up at him. "I think you should go."

"And I appreciate that, but this is where I want to be."

His fingers came underneath my chin. Using them, he tipped them in the direction of his mouth. "Now, just relax. You're getting yourself all worked up when everything is fine. Let Deanna do her job and let me be here. Let me be here with you."

After giving me a chaste kiss, he pulled back, then retrieved my menu for me. I tried to ignore the fact that his agent was currently handling something *huge* for his career, but he was determined to simply focus on having lunch with me.

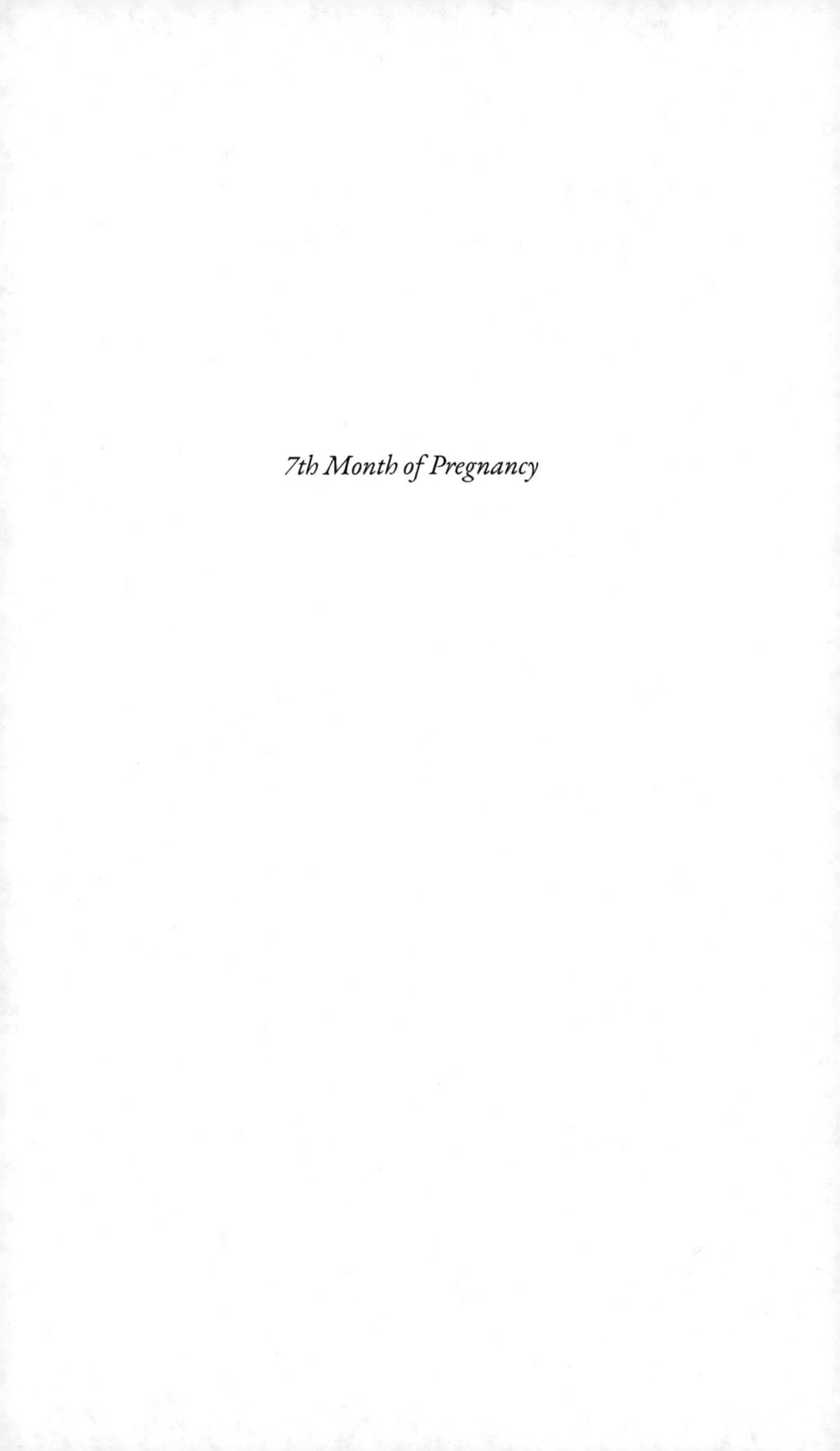

7th Month of Pregnancy

Six

ROXIE

I THINK it was just into the start of my third trimester that I really started to feel it—the stress. However, I could safely say it had nothing to do with my pregnancy.

I jumped, the whirl of a buzz saw the accompaniment of my afternoon on the patio. I'd taken my laptop out there, trying to get some work done since I was officially on maternity leave. Though I still had the office send me any new leads for clientele. Just because I wasn't there, didn't mean I couldn't have my hands on whatever was placed on our approved vendor list. Athletes came to *us* for referrals and *Rox Inc.* aka my staff and myself, had to make sure we had the best of the best to work with them. That's what our consulting firm did.

Usually, I met with each say, new agent or lawyer before they were added to my company's name bank of trusted sources, but with my current condition, globe-trotting what could quite easily sometimes be the *world*, as I had international vendors as well, wasn't as easy as it used to be. In fact, I had stopped all that pretty much at month six, easily tuckered out with all the running I used to do. Like I said, sometimes I traveled internationally, scouting the best of the best as our clients, our athletes deserved that.

Had my job been mostly sedentary I could have stayed active longer, but unfortunately, with the effort and time I did put into this ship I ran, there was no working the sometimes sixty-hour weeks I put in. I also wanted to enjoy the pregnancy, and since I had the means to be away, I decided to do just that—be away.

I had assistants doing the meet-ups for me now, but I only allowed that for a handful of new vendors. I didn't want to add too many new professionals on this way. I wanted to make sure these people were on the up and up, and though I trusted my staff, *I* needed to meet with each new professional personally.

Pushing the lists of potential vendors that I'd been emailed that morning to the side, I decided to work on charity things and where the money my company often donated was going.

That was until my friend, the buzz saw made its reappearance.

A *buzz, buzz* from behind me made my eyes close as I let out a breath. Turning to look behind me from my seat of patio chair, I caught the eye of one of Troy's crew through the window. He lifted his hand, waving at me with a work-gloved hand.

Giving him my best smile, I waved back. Usually, when Troy came to check up on things, they kept the noise down in the baby's room, but without him, as a buffer, they went to work. I'd have to get them some lemonade or something soon so they'd take a break.

It worked last time as far as the noise.

The guy lowered his hand and the buzzing hit again.

Shaking my head, I went back to work on my budget spreadsheet, typing, and clicking.

But then the hammering started.

Nails drove into whatever surface they were hitting behind me, and the once calming waves of the Miami beach before me grew to be a distance memory. I couldn't even enjoy the smell anymore, the sand and ocean breeze pushed aside in favor of my other heightened sense—my ears.

Only a few more days. Just a few more days.

Completion of the nursery couldn't come soon enough and I stretched my fingers out, trying to push through the noise.

"Roxie?"

Awareness pulsed through me again. I jumped and my laptop, already on the unsteady surface of my lap, fell.

With a quick hand, Ms. Harris got it, spry for what I knew to be the age of sixty-one.

Getting the device, she righted it on my lap. "I'm sorry, dear. I didn't mean to frighten you."

No, she didn't frighten me.

She scared the shit out of me.

How is that woman always so dang quiet?

Getting my heart to calm, I turned, gazing up at her. "I'm fine. Fine."

She folded her hands in front of her stretchy, floral printed pants. "You must have been very focused."

I had been trying. I smiled a little. "What's up?"

"It's just after one. Now, that your lunch has settled it's time for your vitamins and afternoon activity."

Oh, Jesus.

I made sure to keep my smile, knowing this routine all too well. But I really was trying to get something done today.

I held my laptop. "Do you think we can maybe *skip* the activity today? Or maybe just move it to a little later today? I was in the middle of something."

And really, I didn't feel like getting down on all fours and doing exercises. I knew they were good for the baby and me, but still.

Ms. Harris shrugged a little. "We can move it. But you do know I leave early today."

"Oh really?" I asked intrigued. I was *a lot* intrigued actually. I could get the afternoon off from schedules and Ms. Harris.

She nodded. "Griffin will be in this evening, remember? I'm not needed. If you wait, you can do the activity with him."

Christ. If I let him, he'd have me on all fours all night, and not in the way I would want. He had last time he did mommy aerobics with me.

He'd been really anal about those things lately, keeping me happy, healthy. He wasn't here all the time due to his busy working schedule, but when he was here, he was *here*. Like really, drill sergeant here.

In the back of my mind, I knew all the hubbub in regards to my health was for the same reason I went on maternity leave so early. He wanted the best for me and the baby.

A buzzing hit my ears again, and I closed my eyes, letting the sounds seep through me. This was more of his doing, the nursery, and though I appreciated the gesture, loved it and him...

I can't do this. I can't.

I opened my eyes. "Ms. Harris, I think you can go ahead and take off now. I can handle the vitamins and activity."

I needed to get out of here.

Upon walking into *Rox Inc.* later that afternoon, I turned quite a few heads, but it had nothing to do with the fact I was seven months pregnant.

"Roxie?" One of our staff secretaries widened her eyes, her

black nail-polished fingers touching her throat. "Nice to see you?"

Yes, the words came out as a question and rightly so. I hadn't set foot in the establishment in weeks since I was *technically* on maternity leave.

Try telling the contractors at my house that.

Smiling at her, I simply told her I forgot a few things at my desk. I didn't want questions. I just wanted a place to work.

Ponytail high and bangs just above curly lashes, she nodded, letting me pass her and step down the white marble floors dusted in sparkle embellishments.

The walls of *Rox Inc.* were sleek, clean with a hint of black accents on the walls. The sconces were textured in that color, too, and curved at the bottom with electrical lighting. The place was modern, but also quite pretty with fresh pink flowers decorating the lobby and the desks. I used to pick them myself and bring them in until we started bringing in enough cash flow to hire a florist to handle fresh arrangements.

The thing about my business was even though Griffin provided the startup I wanted to be self-sufficient. Every dime we made went right back, and soon, the place held its own past the loan Griffin provided and then some. I was super proud of this place, so leaving even for the briefest time I had was a struggle.

Feeling at home, I waddled deep within on my short heels. Just because I was hiding out here didn't mean I wasn't going to look professional at my place of work. I passed a few more staff on the way to my corner office, evading questions, yes, but I also had a question of my own.

"Is Stevie here?" I asked, already starting to pull my laptop out of my shoulder bag.

In all black, Tyler, who I knew to be one of the interns here leaned out from behind his computer monitor.

"I believe she stepped out," he said. "Do you want me to call her for you?"

Oh, God no. I didn't need to hear it from her that I was here. My second in command would never let me hear the end of it.

Waving my hand, I told him no matter, and like a dear, he came over and opened the double doors of my office for me.

"You look great, Mrs. Chandler," he said, giving me a small smile.

I laughed, knowing I had to look anything but good after the morning I had. That was nice of him to say so though. Joking, I told him flattery would get him everywhere in this business, and that made him laugh. He left me to my peace, and I stepped into my sanctuary.

Griffin had helped me decorate my little piece of the world, black granite desk, and large oval windows. I wanted him to have a piece of this place too. I wanted to be reminded of him whenever I was in it.

A picture of the two of us sat on my desk, one of our engagement photos, and I really did feel at home, plopping into my conference chair. And plop, I did.

My feet swollen, I took a minute to catch my breath.

It took all I had to get Ms. Harris to let me go. I'd been under her care since the day I hired her, and she kept me on quite a short leash these days.

Sighing, I spread out, but I think I only got my device booted before my door shot open.

Stevie in all her edgy glory made her way into my office. Her curvy hips wrapped in a pencil skirt, she swayed her way into my office. Her six-inch stilettos only added to a frame that already went on forever. She used to model in the plus size industry, a fabulous size twenty-two.

Her arms crossed over her chest as her blonde hair swept over her brown cheeks.

Smirking, she laughed a little. "Griffin, is going to kill you, you know?"

My eyes could only lift to the heavens. Sliding on my chair wheels, I got my spreadsheet open. "Well, he's not going to find out I'm *here* now is he?"

"I've been told to report if such a thing occurs," she simply said, making her way into the room.

Of course she was. I guess because my husband knew me.

I groaned. "I couldn't be at home because there's the contractors working on the baby's room, and then that woman he made me hire."

My mind whirled at the constant scheduling, the *babying* and how my entire day was completely planned. The woman had a specific time for everything and a precise way in which I had to do what she asked. Apparently "nannying" extended to the mother until the baby was born.

I put my hand on Jackson. "She's driving me *crazy*. Her name is Ms. Harris, and she's always in my face with something. I need to eat. I need to sleep. I need to take my vitamins and do my activities."

"Activities?" Stevie chuckled, taking the edge of my desk when she took a seat.

"I wish I was joking. I do mommy aerobics, which is fine, but she also has me doing knitting and sewing. 'All things that aren't bad to learn, Roxie.'"

My Ms. Harris voice nearly had Stevie rolling off my desk, but I wasn't joking. I'd hear it all whenever I complained I didn't feel like or have time to do something.

"All I want is some peace and quiet," I explained to Stevie. I sat back in my chair. "I have to sneak work in at home before Griffin gets in. He wants me to relax, and I get that but..."

Exasperated, I faced out the window. So bright, the Miami sunshine cast a glow over the entire metropolitan area. Downtown had always been so busy, so lovely. That's why I had my office here.

I turned back to Stevie. "I'm pregnant, but I'm not disabled. I think he forgets that."

As if someone knew, he bumped me, lodging a limb into the wall of my stomach. My blouse poked at the *bump*, and I laughed a little.

It was so crazy I could *feel* him, his presence beyond that of his flutters. He really was in there, my baby boy, my Jackson.

Stevie's lip went into her mouth with her smile upon seeing me rub my tummy. Crossing her legs, she tilted her head at me. "Griffin just wants what's best for you, Roxie. What's best for you and the baby?"

I knew he did, which was why being frustrated at all made no sense. He did want what was best. He did.

Stevie placed a pump on the floor. "I won't tell him—this time. But I better not see you in here again before that little one is due."

If there was ever a reason I could doubt why I hired that woman, there wouldn't be now. She was my saving grace. Giving me a wink, she backed away and closed the double doors behind her.

I didn't waste a moment, typing away. I went through my mental to-do list of tasks I had all while paying attention to the time. Ms. Harris was right about one thing today. Griffin would be home soon, and I didn't want to have to cover for myself.

"She's not here, miss. I'm sorry."

I looked up, tilting my head. I couldn't see through the crack of my double doors, but I knew the voice to be Stevie's.

"But I saw her come in. Please. I took the bus all the way here."

That... That voice.

"Can you just ask if she'll see prospective clients?"

I stood slowly, my heart racing, literally slamming against my chest.

My limbs felt heavy, a fiery burn pushing bile up into my throat. It sat there in an angry ball, choking me and not allowing my lungs to find air.

I gripped the desk, the rise of a fainting spell fast approaching. I faced the door, shaking my head.

No. It can't be. Can it?

"I'm sorry you traveled so far, but Mrs. Chandler is simply not seeing clients today. Now, you can leave your name—"

"But you admit she's here. Please. I know her. If you could just ask if she'd see me."

She knows me.

My legs, so shaky took me to the door. Nausea turned its ugly head, and my stomach rolled. Any other time, I'd worry. I'd worry it was the baby or something... that something was wrong. But it wasn't the baby. No, it was her, that woman outside my office.

That voice.

"What's your name, miss?" Stevie asked, her back turning toward me. I knew because I'd opened the door. I knew because I could see her, and then, she could see me when she turned. Someone else turned as well when she did—someone with long, raven-colored hair, and eyes big and brown, as well as beautiful. They were like I remembered, but a bit different now. *She* was a bit different now.

Her hair so lovely, she had the strands messy and up on her head and her tanned skin—a deep copper, flushed. There was also no makeup on a face I was so used to seeing done up.

My inventory was done and I noticed she was holding onto something as her hands fell firmly to her waist. I knew that position well, though, barely a nub could be seen under her shirt. It was a protective position. She was protecting something, someone.

Those brown eyes flashed at me—the black lashes so lengthy.

"Roxie?" she said, and I drew in a breath. I couldn't say her name. It wouldn't form on my lips.

My former step-sister's name.

The Past

Seven

A PINK, pointy flat tapped the heel of my sneaker, and I lowered my book to my lap, dropping my other foot to the floor from the bench I sat on.

Cassidy's skirted-hip touched the side of the dressing room I'd been hiding in, her arms crossed over her chest. Her lashes did a flickering thing, eyes full of judgment over my book, but then she smiled.

She pushed her bangs from in front of her eyes, then tipped her chin. "You're hiding."

I was.

"I'm not," I lied, tucking the book underneath me. I had just gotten to the good part, but wouldn't dare dwell on that. She might look at me funny if she knew I was having a better time in here. Even worse she might think I wasn't normal. I didn't want her thinking I wasn't normal.

I sat up, and Cassidy came in, smelling of freesia and other flowery things. She tried to get me to wear that stuff all the time, and I did like it, but it could be overpowering.

She touched a dress still hung up on the wall, then eyed me over it when she picked it up. "You don't like it?"

I stood, wishing I could lie to her. I had never been good at lying, though.

I shook my head, and she took my hand, dragging me out of the dressing room and into the busy storefront. Everyone was here today, kids from school and what not. It was the last shopping weekend before homecoming. I guess that had been why.

Cassidy worked her way around the store, her cloak of dark hair twisted into a thick braid down her back. Mine matched. She'd done it for me before we left the house today.

She turned around a gown in her hand that could only be known as a frock. She bit her lip a little.

"It's pretty," she said, pulling her long fingers through the material at the bottom. It bunched all weird and had this sequency stuff in a pale pink color. The first one she picked out had been similar. It wasn't like she didn't have any taste, but we just... didn't have many options.

I wasn't as easy to fit as she was.

Trying hard to hide my distaste for the dress, I went to take it, but Cassidy knew me too well. I knew her, too.

She shoved the dress back into the rack before I could take it, shaking her head as she did.

She put her hands on my shoulders. "We're going to find you something."

Honestly, I wondered why she continued to bother. I was kind of humoring her today. It wasn't like I had a date for the dance or anything. I never did. This was my dad. My dad told me I should come today.

Her fingers threaded in mine, she tugged me to the four or so racks designated to essentially *my* part of the store. The plus size section wasn't ever really big.

Cassidy thumbed and thumbed, so determined, and I turned over my shoulder, looking for Radha. I found her quickly, tossing gowns over her shoulder. She and the other girls we came with today held dresses up to their fronts in the other section of the store, spinning around with them and giggling.

Radha's dark eyes found mine while holding a green one. Flashing away quickly, she grinned at her friends, showcasing the low back of the gown she held. She'd been acting so different lately, ever since we started high school.

"I got it," came from behind me and I turned, not confident about another Cassidy find.

But then... I saw it.

It was black and stopped mid-calf with ruched fabric at the bottom. The top itself looked like a heart, the waist so tiny.

"A sweetheart neckline," Cassidy said bringing her fingers over the top of each of the heart's curve. She gave me that wide smile again. She was always smiling. I guess I would, too. She was so pretty.

I found my way into the dressing room by her hand, humoring her once more with this dress she found. I had tried on so many today. It just wasn't my thing.

"Just try, sweet pea."

My dad's voice in my head, I slid the gown on, getting the back zipped up pretty good without help. In actuality only the very tip of the zipper I couldn't get up.

"You got it, Roxie?"

I came out so she wouldn't come in. I did get the dress zipped so she wouldn't have to help me.

Out of the room, I stood there, waiting for some kind of response from Cassidy. She hadn't said anything when I stepped out, simply staring at me.

And she wasn't the only one.

It seemed as if the world had stopped around me in that moment. Quite literally, people stopped, stared. Girls wearing their own gowns remained silent, as well as the employees passing more off to them. They all stopped. They stopped and looked at me.

Feeling vulnerable, I made the moves to go back into the dressing room. I made the mistake of not looking in the mirror before I came out.

I probably look like an idiot.

Cassidy caught my fingers before I could leave, though, quicker than me.

"You must see," she said, dragging me by the hand. But I didn't want to see. I didn't if I looked...

I caught myself in a set of long mirrors outside the dressing room, my fingers to a bodice of what seemed to be a trim waist, black material flaring over my hips before sweeping out and flowing. The silk wrapped tight around my waist, but not too tight. It fit snug, pushing up my chest just a little. My shoulders were exposed, but that was okay. I didn't mind it.

My glasses were slid from my face, Cassidy's doing, and I watched myself in the mirror, my round face and big eyes. But they didn't look big. *I* didn't look big. I looked proportionate. I looked like this was all right, this dress all right for me.

"You can wear this with your Converses, too," Cassidy said in my ear. I could see her grinning from my side through the mirror and she was right, my shoes did match.

I tipped my sneaker out to verify, smiling when I turned to look at Cassidy. I had caught someone else's gaze before I did, though, and that someone was wearing something very similar.

The dress covered Radha well, too, but just in a different way. My step-sister had always been svelte, trim, and the gown highlighted all that. Her bust sat perfect, her waist so small.

I think Cassidy noticed at the same time I had on what her sister wore. She stepped back, letting Radha into our circle, and a circle had formed, the three of us and Radha's friends.

Radha's mouth opened slowly, her eyes flicking back from me to her in the mirror.

I turned toward her, feeling weird all the sudden.

"It looks good on you, Rad," I said because it did. It did look good.

Haley, Radha's friend with red hair, tilted her head in the mirror. "Yeah, but it looks better on you."

Blinking, I didn't expect that, especially from her friend.

I lifted my hands. "I..."

"She's right," Radha said, surprising me more. Her gaze went back to the pair of us in the mirror, and she stared. She stared at us such a long time.

Her lashes flicked away from me and she smiled before facing her friends. "I guess she *fills* it in ways I don't."

A laugh sounded a little behind her words, and that summoned more, more laughter, her friends and some of our other classmates who stood to watch. Of course, they stopped to watch my step-sister who was so popular at school.

The sound shrunk me in my place, my fingers sweating, and my heart feeling funny. I didn't want to be in the dress anymore. I—

Cassidy reached out, reached to touch my arm. I knew because I saw the move in the mirror. That was the only way I knew, though. She never made contact. She retreated, choosing not to.

Her hand falling back to her side, she left me standing there, breaking eye contact with me through the mirror.

Radha turned, her hair sweeping over her shoulder. She didn't wear a braid like Cassidy and me. She stopped wearing those.

"Take the dress," she said to me, her hands on her hips. "No big deal I guess."

But it did feel like a big deal.

It did.

Eight

ROXIE - AGE FIFTEEN

"Is Radha mad at me?"

Cassidy took the seat beside me, sliding underneath the back table I'd been sitting at. I sat here nearly all night, choosing to do so by myself underneath the flashing lights.

The whole room had been decked out, beautiful for the homecoming dance. The student council had done a good job, adding streamers and things to the gym. They even put glitter on the tables.

Cassidy rested her hands on the decorated tablecloth, leaning in. "What makes you think that, Roxie?"

My gaze lifted, finding Radha and her friends. She'd stayed with them all night tonight, came here with them instead of with Cassidy and me. She and her posse let it go on the dance floor, the DJ's favorites as he pointed at them behind his turntable. The little high school dance floor was consumed with people, but Radha and her friends had everyone's attention. She wore a green dress tonight, opting to piece it with a fringy sash and jewels pressed to her forehead. She looked like a princess. My stepmom, Julie, said she looked like her at her first dance. She'd helped them both get ready tonight, Radha and Cassidy. She donned up their traditional homecoming gowns with elements from their Indian heritage. They had a good time, laughing and everything, and Julie had invited me to be a part of it. It just didn't feel like my place.

I put my hands in my lap, on the skirt of my black dress. I shrugged.

"She's just acting differently," I said, thinking about the incident at the dress shop. She'd never said anything like that to me before. She'd never made fun of me before.

I shook my head. "Is she mad about the dress thing?" Because I didn't want to get it. I didn't if it made her mad at me. I didn't even want to go to this stupid dance. Things like that didn't matter to me, but she did.

She mattered.

Cassidy's hand went over mine in my lap. She picked out a pink dress, a sash like Radha's wrapped around her.

She squeezed. "Just don't think about it. Just…"

Her gaze drifted off toward the dance floor, and mine followed. Like Radha knew eyes were on her, she spotted the pair of us staring at her. She stopped dancing then, slowing away from the beat she danced to with her friends.

"She's fine," Cassidy said, staring at her. "I'm sure she is."

I had to take her word for it I guess. She did know her better than me, her sister by blood and not marriage.

Cassidy's hand stayed in my lap, and the pair of us sat there for a bit, silent aside from the heavy dance track in the room. Though quiet, I didn't feel alone like I had before. It was Cassidy. Her hand rubbing mine, she had always been there for me. She never left. She hadn't *changed* as Radha seemed to. And she did change.

I just didn't understand why.

I got closer to my step-sister, almost feeling like I was mourning another. We'd been so close since our parents married, and I truly did feel like I lost her, but then, something happened with the change of the music. The song got louder, the music pumped at the max, and Radha broke away from her friends. She *left* her friends, and came to me.

Out of breath, she arrived at Cassidy and my table.

My hand slowly left Cassidy's. "Rad—"

"You guys coming out?" she asked, but I didn't know if she was serious. But she was smiling, though. She smiled completely wide.

Her hand came out, reaching for mine and I stood, letting her help me up.

My lips parted, I faced Cassidy, a similar grin, as her sister's on her face. She mouthed something to me in dark room, and I deciphered the words, "Told you."

Her hand joined mine after that, and together, the three of us got up and joined Radha's friends. They were already there on the dance floor, having a good time, and I got in there, too. It was rather easy to follow the dance moves, the singer calling them out before they happened, but that's not what made the whole experience easy, fun.

I raised my arms, dancing with my sisters as they surrounded me with their friends. We hadn't had a moment together like this in a long time. We hadn't, and I never wanted it to end.

The song ended too soon, but Radha's hands came out again, holding mine and making me move with her. I did, dancing and Cassidy clapped alongside us, throwing her own arms up on occasion. We danced two more songs that way, all fast, but then the DJ surprised us. He let me down with a slow song.

The guys seemed to come out of nowhere, asking Radha's friends to dance. Radha had a partner, too, and Cassidy got one next.

Feeling I should, I went to walk off the dance floor. It just seemed like the most natural thing to do since I didn't get asked to dance, but then I heard Radha's voice.

"Roxie?"

I stopped. Her arms were still around her date, a tall guy with dark hair. I knew him to be a football player at our school. Radha always dated the jocks when she did.

She came over, taking my arm. "You should dance with Kevin's brother, Brian."

Kevin was the guy she'd been dancing with, and Radha pointed, gesturing to a tall guy by the punch table. He looked very similar to Kevin, large build, and dark hair, and I knew him to be just as popular. He played sports, too, soccer I think.

I shrugged. "I..."

"Oh, come on," she said, taking my hand, and then she did the worst thing. She started to *take* me toward this guy, this guy who was so beautiful.

My feet skidded. "Radha, no."

"But he wants to."

And that made me stop, pause. "He doesn't."

"He *does*," she said, nodding. "Kevin told me. Why do you think I'm taking you to him?"

I didn't believe her. It just... it just seemed too weird. I think I would have noticed someone like him watching me. I would have noticed, but then he came closer, leaving his punch cup on a table as Radha gestured him over.

My heart pushed into that tiny space, the one I was supposed to breathe from but couldn't all the sudden, and then he was in front of me, a tall, gorgeous guy, and I couldn't breathe. I couldn't think. I just wanted to run. I didn't want to be here anymore. This was a mistake.

"Brian this is Roxie," she said. "My sister."

Her sister.

I looked up at this guy who was even more perfect up

close. He had these lips that were full and curved subtly in the corners, and he had the curliest lashes.

He placed his hand out to take mine. "Hi, Roxie. I'm Brian."

My hand disappeared in his own, shaking it slowly.

"Roxie," I said, my breathing so rapid.

I felt myself being pushed from behind after that. Heck, he was, too. We were being pushed together, the pair of us by Radha and one of her friends. Before I knew it, Brian and I were out on the dance floor, my hands in both of his.

But then, they weren't, one of his large hands on the small of my back.

He guided me into him, into the dance, and we ended up by his brother, and my... my sister. They were both there, Radha and Cassidy with their dance partners beside us.

I couldn't breathe again, but this time it wasn't bad.

We danced through that whole song, Brian and I, and we chatted a little, too. He was actually a junior, which felt so crazy to me. I was only a freshman, and I was dancing with him. He was dancing with me, and he wanted to.

We got punch together later that night, and his fingers came up to touch mine, my hand on my drink cup.

He brushed my fingers softly, delicately, and made my belly do all kinds of weird things. They felt like such good things.

He leaned in, smelling like cologne. Like something, my dad or someone older would wear.

"Can I kiss you?" he asked me, and things got so tight in my chest. I felt like I was suffocating and breathing at the same time.

He took my free hand before I could answer him and we went some place, behind a curtain. The photographer took pictures in front of it earlier tonight. He slid my empty cup from me, using his fingers to bring me closer by the waist. He was going to kiss me. He wanted to kiss me.

I had never been kissed.

His lips got so close, warm as the distance between us wasn't far. He dampened them, moving to close the distance even more, but I stepped back. I didn't know why.

Pulling back, Brian tilted his head. He didn't say anything, but his eyes shifting told of his confusion. His confusion of me, an oddity. Why wouldn't a girl want to kiss him? He was so beautiful, so much more than me.

Emotions rushed me at the way he looked at me, whatever thoughts or conclusions he'd *made* about me, and the thickest sea of panic hit my chest, fear.

As well as embarrassment.

Feeling the influx of it, I made moves to go around him, leave. All of this was too much for me. I wasn't ready for all this kissing. I just...

We crashed into each other on my way around him, and he dropped my cup, the paper rolling away.

I dipped, patting it on all fours, and that's when I heard the laughter and gasps.

Gazing up, I saw Radha, as well as a few of her friends and others from our class around her. They all stared, though, not at me.

They looked ahead, above me.

I turned and saw something I didn't understand. Brian was there, but not how I left him. He had his pants lowered a little, adjusting like he was trying to hurry and get them up.

He managed to do so, re-zipping his fly and buckling his belt next. After he had gotten himself together, he passed me, mumbling, "Thanks, sweetheart" before passing Radha and my classmates.

"I didn't know you were into doing *that*, Roxie," came a voice. It was my sister's, Radha's.

Smiling, she crossed her arms over her chest, her head tilted. I didn't understand the smile. Nothing was funny.

It only felt cruel.

As well as her laughter when it started, her friends slowly behind. The only person who didn't laugh was Cassidy.

She stood there, seemingly singularly. She watched the scene unfold and said nothing, nor did she do anything. She left me alone, the laughter around us.

The tears burning my eyes, I went to stand, my palms black from the floor, my pretty dress wrinkled and dirty. And I did feel dirty; I couldn't help it considering what Brian did, what he insinuated happened between us.

Heads back, Radha and her crew laughed their way away from me. They took everything away, my arms shaking as I remained on all fours. I wanted to get up, but I couldn't. I couldn't find the strength. I could only look at the floor, then let the tears fall, as the last remaining pair of shoes stepped away from me, going away with Radha and her crew. They were a pair of pink heels.

They matched her pointy-toed flats.

The Present

Nine

GRIFFIN

I GOT HOME a little later than expected, the house dark outside except for the outdoor lights illuminating the driveway and the entryway's outdoor sconce. I'd been invited to stay out longer; drinks passed my way by businessmen. I had been offered the deal of the century, a role in Roddy Price's new feature film and it wasn't just a cameo.

A spot for an athlete had been reserved to partner alongside the main lead, a well-known actor already cast in the role. The actor would be playing, of all things, a doctor of sports medicine and the athlete was needed in more of a sidekick role to him. The athlete also had a healthy speaking part.

I auditioned a few weeks back for it, and well, I must have been good enough because they offered me the gig today. It turned out, Deanna had been right that day on the golf course. I had been vetted. In fact, one of the first to audition.

I shook my head at the thought, unable to wait to tell Roxie. She knew about the audition and role. But she didn't know about this, the news of me getting the role fresh as of today.

She'd probably be in bed judging by the hour. I did try to

hurry home to her but had to stay after my new director/ producer offered me such a huge break. While those drinks were being passed, I kept my eyes on the time, declining the drinks myself and just being there for the celebration. I thought about checking in on Roxie several times but didn't want to bug her too much. It felt like I was always checking in on her these days, the closer the baby was to being born the main reason, yes, but in the back of my mind, I knew so much more. She hadn't mentioned seeing her counselor again, but that didn't mean she wasn't.

Trying not to think about that, I unlocked the door, the house dormant, dark. I placed my keys on the hook by the door and took my ball cap off, tossing it on top of the coat rack by the door. I left my shoes there as well and made my way through the house. Furniture and other refurbishments we'd done over the few years we lived here greeted my way and I couldn't wait to do more. I hoped to have many years in this home and build more on it with Roxie.

Making my way down the hallway, I had to stop at one of those builds that were currently in progress. I flicked on the light and the room filled with yellows, whites, and grays.

I stepped into what would be Jackson's room, and though there were still tools there, wood and other spare parts, I could see it. I could see *us* here, the three of us.

I made my way over to the changing table—a hand carved rocking chair right next to it. That had been a gift from my pop. He hand delivered it himself after we made the announcement to the family so many months ago. Not many things could get that man on a plane, but he did just the feat. He did that for his first grandson.

The beautiful piece of furniture went so well in here. It made it feel woodsy, fitting the owl theme that Troy did for Roxie's baby shower. She really loved owls, and they made their way in here, on the walls and on the night-lights. Thick, wide curtains draped down the back wall, coming together and either keeping the light in or and out.

In front of it all, on display for the world to see was a crib.

Holding onto the wooden bar of it brought some kind of emotion out of me. My son would be sleeping here in a matter of months.

My son.

I picked up the soft, mini basketball in the crib, holding it tight. I wanted to see him and his mom.

I have to at least hold her for a little while. I'll be quiet.

I returned the ball to the crib and left the room, clicking the light off behind me and closing the door. I made my way down the hall and was surprised to see another light shining from underneath the door.

She's still up.

My lips lifted into a small smile. Picking up my pace, I made it to our bedroom, catching Roxie immediately. She lay partially underneath the covers, the low back of her pale blue nightgown allowing me to see the expanse of her creamy brown skin. Laying on her side, she had a book in her hand, which could be seen peeking above her shoulder. She must have been reading with only the end table light illuminating the room.

I tapped the doorframe, alerting her to my presence.

"Knock, knock," I said, coming in and she turned a little, only ever so slightly. I got to her before she could make the full rotation, drawing my shirt off along the way.

"I missed you today," I told her, pushing my arms around her, the baby. Her book fell from her fingers, hitting the floor with a *thump*, but I wouldn't let her pick it up.

I bought her close, kissing her and smelling her skin. I told her I loved her as I buried my nose into her neck and waited to hear her voice. I didn't care what she said in response. I just wanted to hear it, hear her. What I didn't expect, though? What I never wanted to expect?

The sound of her tears.

Audible, it came lightly, but steadfast, constant. Pushing Roxie on her back, I had her turn for me and her eyes... they were the damn saddest I'd ever seen.

"Roxie?" I touched her cheek, and then...

Panic. It couldn't be helped by what I saw, my wife in tears with her hand on her stomach. The dread reared its ugly head and socked me in the gut like a blow to the chest during one of my games.

I covered both her cheeks.

"What's wrong?" I asked. I urged. Instinctually, my hand went to the bundle between us. Afraid to touch her, put pressure there, I declined and sat up instead.

I reached into my pocket.

"I'll call the doctor. Tell me what's wrong—"

"No," she said, making eye contact with me. She'd been lost for a minute, out of it and more tears fell when she shook her head.

"It's not... I mean, I'm not... the baby is fine. Jackson's fine."

I lowered my phone, but the ache in her voice didn't do much to relieve any panic, panic for our child, panic for her.

I put the phone on the bed. "What's going on...?"

But she didn't let me finish. She simply turned into my side with our baby and when she did.

She sobbed into my chest.

The tears came hot, hard and her whole body shook from the influx.

My arms coming around her, I felt that shake, those intense tremors flowing throughout her limbs. The existence caused a fear to run rapidly within me. In fact, I'd only remembered such fear one other time. It had been when we first moved here.

When I thought I'd lost her.

I held her close now, not understanding the tears, her pain.

"Roxie?" But she wouldn't speak. She only cried into me.

So I let her, holding her until she was ready until she *could* tell me. I never rushed Roxie. She always came back to me in time, always.

I waited so long, patiently, and when the words did come, I almost missed them. They'd been so soft.

"I'm so mad," she said as she finally spoke. "I'm so angry at myself."

Confused, I drew back, reaching to place a hand on her cheek. I saw the anger that ran deep within her green eyes.

I swept a thumb over her cheek. "What's making you upset?"

I still didn't understand and she blinked, taking herself away from me.

She moved her fingers underneath her eyes.

"I let her get to me, Griffin," she said, tears running so heavily down her cheeks. She blinked some away, but that didn't stop them.

"Who?" I asked her. I'd never seen her this way.

She answered my question after that and never in my life would I have ever been ready for what she told me.

"Cassidy," she said, lifting her head to look at me. "My ex-step-sister."

Ten

GRIFFIN

MY MERCEDES FLEW the next morning, probably going faster than I should have upon getting off the ferry into town. I never usually took the vintage sports car out, but I needed to get somewhere quickly, needed to get *back* quickly. I only had so many hours before my wife woke up and I planned to be there for her.

Unlike other parties had in the past.

"I hope it all gets worked out," Stevie, Roxie's assistant, said in my ear. I had my Bluetooth headset on and had since getting off the ferry.

After telling her I hoped so, too, I ended the call, pulling my finger away from the earpiece. I called Stevie, Roxie's co-worker, hoping and praying she had some information on the woman who came in to see Roxie.

Her step-sister.

Shaking my head, I *still* couldn't believe the reality of what sent me out today.

But then again, I had the evidence in my hands last night, hadn't I? My wife in my hands...

"She came in for something. To see me for something..."
Roxie had said last night, sniffling.

This had been *after* she cried herself out, her eyes red, and
I'd never *un*-see that sight. It burned into my brain, her pain. It
always had.

My hands gripped the wheel as I zipped through morning
traffic, gratefully dormant, as it was so early. I knew exactly
where I was going. My car had an excellent navigation system
installed a while back. The specific address I was going to only
had to be put in.

That's where Stevie came through.

She had gotten the woman's address at Roxie's office
yesterday. In fact, from what Stevie told me, Roxie's *ex*-step-
sister had pretty much forced it on her. The woman did want
to see Roxie.

It didn't matter how much she didn't want to see her.

"I left," Roxie had told me in my arms. *"I don't know what
she wanted with me. I just left. I couldn't see her. I couldn't
take it..."*

As it turned out, after Roxie had left, Stevie forced the
woman out. She'd told me as much. She must have picked up
on Roxie's queues, her reaction to her, her step-sister.

I knew I liked Roxie's assistant. She had a good head on
her shoulders. She was a great supplement to my wife and gave
her the support she both needed and deserved for her business.
In this case, Stevie had handled a situation and done so in a
way far better than I could have. I never thought rationally
when it came to Roxie, when it came to her in pain.

I breathed, trying to get some semblance of a clear head
before walking into the situation I traveled toward. But that
was made harder with every word that lingered in my head
from last night and only made worse by what I got from Stevie
this morning. The address hadn't been the only thing Stevie
got from the woman or at least speculated about.

The woman had been holding her belly when she came to see Roxie, a little nub, and that only put things into perspective for me, as well as infuriate the hell out of me.

Neither of the girls had apparently known the reason why this woman went to see Roxie. Stevie had kicked her out after getting her address, and well, Roxie had left well before. But considering the situation, Roxie and my situation, the woman's reasoning, at least *to me* anyway, seemed crystal clear.

It was no mystery that Roxie and I were doing all right, the last few years a blessing for us with the opportunities we'd been given, and if that woman knew that and was pregnant on top...

I pulled up to a house, a blur as to how I even got there. I had to have followed the GPS' commands, but I had no recollection, my vision nothing but red.

Finding a number on the mailbox outside, I confirmed the address, turning off my car. After getting out, I shut the door, trying to keep calm, my body literally shaking to do it. But how could I? How could that be managed when I was about to approach the very person who'd caused my wife such heartache in the past? Roxie had told me stories, enough about her previous stepfamily to understand the reality of what they put her through.

The woman who came to see Roxie yesterday, Cassidy, had pretty much tortured my wife with verbal beatings *for years*, Cassidy's sister Radha, the ringleader. She had been the worse, but the two had been a strong pair, one feeding into the other, the weaker one, Cassidy. And then there had been Roxie's old stepmother, the absolute worse from what I understood.

The trio had been a motley crew of insults both passive and overt, dragging Roxie through the mud whenever they could. They picked on her, poked *at her*, someone who'd already been through so much. Roxie's momma had killed herself, her dad remarrying very quickly. From what I understood, he did so to help his daughter by providing a family unit for her, not knowing the ultimate result.

Knowing the reality of that chilling result, I couldn't believe I was here to approach one of those very people who'd hurt her. Before she'd been kicked out of Roxie's office, Stevie told me, Cassidy had begged to see Roxie, actually pleading, saying she needed her help, saying she needed her.

So where was she when Roxie needed her?

The house I stood before was more than run down, shutters falling from the windows. There was garbage on the lawn and more than enough yelling coming from inside. The smell —sewage or something, burned my lungs as I made my way from my car to the door, and I cringed, disgusted by it. That woman would live in a place like this, and I wondered for how long as well as something else, too.

Had she been watching us? Had she been watching my wife, waiting in the wings to approach her, *take* something from her?

The potential of the thoughts being true absolutely sickened me and my fists hit the door of the house a little too loud for the hour.

So much for being calm.

I hit the door so hard, a burn struck my fist when I pulled away, but I didn't bother to shake it out. I simply hit again until a woman answered—her face dirty, her lips chapped.

Her gaze grilled over me, spotting my car behind me.

I stepped in front of her, cutting off her view. "I'm looking for someone who lives here."

A whistle pulled through her teeth when she sucked at them.

She crossed her arms over a large bust covered in a dirty shirt. "A lot of folks live here."

And from the background noise, I could tell. The arguing simply got louder when she opened the door, kids in the background, too, and from behind her, I could see folks gathered in the kitchen. They ate there, talked, and smoked.

Stepping to the side, she cut off my view this time.

I got out a paper from my pocket, handing it to the woman. I wrote down Cassidy's information this morning from Stevie.

Squinting, the woman read it. Tipping her chin, she called out behind herself.

"Cassidy," she said, turning back my way.

She smoothed her arms back over her chest. "She'll come. She said to get her if anyone comes by for her. She's only been living here a few weeks or so."

That answered my earlier question, but that didn't mean she didn't live in the city for longer.

She could have been watching us for a long time.

Stay calm.

I tried as well as I could, thanking the woman before I distanced myself. I left from in front of the door, going out to the dirty lawn with my hands in my pockets.

Heat in my veins, I could feel myself getting amped up, and the movement in my peripheral vision brought my head up, a woman catching my attention. She couldn't be much older than Roxie and my age of twenty-six, considering she went to high school with Roxie.

But damn did she look it.

She had bags under her eyes, her hair messy and eyes bloodshot like she barely got any sleep last night.

Coming outside, she stepped with hesitant steps, her pink flip-flops stepping into the dirt of the property.

I stared at her with every step she made, stared into the eyes of the woman who caused so much pain. How could someone be so terrible to someone else? How could someone be so hurtful to Roxie in particular? She was so good, kind.

My nostrils flared at who was clearly Cassidy got closer

and hands on her stomach, she clearly cradled something. I hadn't noticed before, so put off by how run down she looked.

The evidence of a bump was clearly there. This woman was pregnant. Not as far along as Roxie, but she was definitely carrying a child.

I took a step back when I felt she was getting too close and that summoned her to stop, dark, black hair flowing over her eyes.

"You're Griffin," she said, and I wasn't surprised she knew who I was. I'd probably been the reason she'd come, sought her previous step-sister out.

No sense in beating around the bush.

"How much?" I asked her, forcing my words to form, slow and calculated. Again, I was trying to check my temper, keep my cool.

Especially since she was pregnant.

Cassidy's mouth parted. She blinked but said nothing.

I pushed air through my nose.

"How much do you want?" I asked, moving my arms over my chest. "That's why you're here, right? That's why you came to her? To Roxie?"

She still played dumb, shaking her head as she pushed hair behind her ear.

She squeezed her stomach, rubbing. "No. That's not why I—"

"Good," I said. "Because you weren't going to get anything. I only came out here to put everything out on the table. To get everything in the open so you'd know."

Dark eyebrows narrowed closer together. "So I'd know what?"

"Where you stand when it comes to my family and me. Roxie wants nothing to do with you and you coming here only started a shit storm that wasn't necessary. I mean, she's pregnant for fuck's sake."

That anger no longer held back. It came in a fury, and I looked away for a moment, squeezing the bridge of my nose.

"I know that," came in front of me and I looked up, a woman so very pregnant with her hands on her own swollen belly.

I dropped my hand. "No contact with her. You don't go to her office, and you don't come by our house. We're not giving you anything. Not you, your sister, or your momma—"

"Please," she said, coming forward. "I don't want your money. I don't want Roxie's money, and my sister and mom don't want anything either. In fact, they don't even know I'm here."

I eyed her, not understanding.

She clued me in.

"I just need to talk to Roxie. I need her help."

Her hands moved, tenderly, lovingly over that swollen bump.

I did that with my own child, my wife's stomach a deep connection between our baby and us.

Cassidy didn't know, but what she'd done only made this whole thing worse. She was using her unborn child to get to me. What kind of person did that?

I guess her.

Disgusted with her even more than I had been when I arrived, I left her, going to my car. I said what I needed to. I was done, but that didn't stop her from following me and later, calling my name when I got behind the wheel of my Mercedes convertible.

I faced her, no more patience. I had a little when I came.

Now, no more.

I pointed at her, all but shaking behind the wheel.

"Stay the hell away," I said, swallowing. "Just say away."

I'd like to say shock took her face.

But my words only seemed to sadden her, her expression falling as she took a step back away from my car.

Unaffected by the expression, I forced my key into the ignition, starting the car. I put the Mercedes into gear, then sped the hell out of there.

I had to be there when my wife woke up.

Eleven

ROXIE

Fatigue writhed throughout my entire body, my eyes especially. I rubbed them, feeling cold when my arms fell from the sheets.

"Griffin?" I questioned, my lids sliding open. They burned so badly. They itched.

God, how did I lose it so quickly?

No one answered my call, and I fell out of my head. Griffin, he was gone.

I pushed up, my arms weighted, drained. I pulled Samson, my body pillow, from my side and up to my chest. I snuggled him and Jackson but wished for something more. I had Griffin's arms around me just this morning. I felt them all night. He'd been there all night with me.

I pushed my hair out of my face, feeling like more than a fool. It had been years since her, since *them*, but it all... It all suddenly felt so fresh.

Sliding to the edge of the bed, I used the bedpost to get up, slipping my bare feet into my house shoes.

Usually, I had a house full of people to worry about,

workers and what have you. But today was Sunday, a day of rest. It also happened to be Ms. Harris' day off. I could relax.

I could recoup.

"Griffin?" I rounded a corner of the house moments later, peering out a window in the hallway to the beach. A few runners hiked their knees during a sprint, our neighbors. I passed the window, circulating the house. I called Griffin most of the way, but like before I heard nothing. I eventually made my way back to the bedroom and grabbed my phone off my end table. He left me no text message. He left no note.

Where is he?

I checked the garage last, my Mini Cooper parked next to his silver Range Rover, but one car was missing.

I stood in the spot of his Mercedes. He never took it out. It was something he drove when he wanted to relax or take us out for the day somewhere.

A chill pulsed through me and I realized I shouldn't be standing out here. I had higher risks now. I had responsibilities with Jackson, so I made my way back to the bedroom. I took a moment to dress, finding a breathable sundress. After zipping it up, I found my phone again, dialing.

My flip-flops creaked on the floorboards as I went out into the foyer. The chandelier above drew in the sun and painted colors on the walls. That's when I spotted him, right out the front window.

I hung up the phone, Griffin's little Mercedes cruising up the driveway.

Confused, I dropped my cell to the lounge by the front door.

Opening up the door, I did so as the garage opened, Griffin's doing when he placed his hand to the button on his car's visor.

He spotted me when he did it, his lashes lowering a little before lifting his hand from the wheel to wave at me. He actually didn't end up going into the garage. He parked outside the door, getting out in a set of stretchy black *Under Armour* and athletic shorts. With his matching sneakers and baseball cap, he looked like he'd just got in from doing a run. We had a local park he'd drive to sometimes, but he'd never take the Mercedes for that.

"Hey. What are you doing out here?" he asked me like it wasn't unusual *he* was out here.

Getting to me, he reached out, but I backed up. He didn't look right, his cheeks all flushed and everything.

I pulled my arm in. "What's going on?"

He had to know this was usual and I think he did right away. I saw it when his eyes averted.

He palmed his keys but didn't answer.

"What. Is. Going. On, Griffin? Where did you go?"

A drawn out breath escaped his lips. Raising his hat, he pushed a hand over flattened blond locks before repositioning it.

His eyes found mine. "Let's go inside."

I crossed my arms, standing my ground. "Let's stay out here."

"Roxie."

"Griffin?"

He sighed, coming forward. "It's important people know they can't bully you. That's why I went out. That's where I went."

My eyes narrowed, confused. "What do you mean?"

His hand went over his mouth, no words falling from his lips, and my heart fluttered a wave. Something wasn't right. Something... felt off.

"Where exactly did you go? What do you mean people need to know they can't—"

"I have to protect you," he said, his jaw working. "And that's what I did today. Now, I don't know exactly what that woman wanted with you yesterday, Roxie, but she needed to know that coming to see you was inappropriate. She knew that after our interaction, and won't do it again."

It all flurried around me, an active blizzard with a chilling current.

I squeezed my arms, feeling that chill again. "You mean Cassidy? Why are you talking about Cassidy? Why are *we* talking about Cassidy, Griff—"

"Because I went to see her," he said, putting his hands on my arms. He squeezed. "I had to. She needed to know and she won't bother you anymore. I made sure of that."

The words ripped through me, sliced and cut sharp like a blade. He went to see her. He went to see my former step-sister. He...

"Why would you do that?" gasped from my throat. It was so dry, cracked. "Why would you actually *talk* to her? Interact with her? I didn't want that. Why would you? How could you?"

I could see the questions hitting him like bullets with his expression, silencing him.

He rubbed my arms. "I had to, baby. Her coming here wasn't okay."

"So, you decided to make that call?" I asked, backing out of his arms. "Take it upon yourself and do something about it?"

"Well, yeah," he said and once again, reached for me. But this time, I didn't let him.

I wouldn't.

His arms went down to his sides. "I had to protect you. I *have* to protect you, both of you. You and Jackson. Baby, I watched you cry for *hours* last night, literally until you fell asleep by something that woman did. You can't expect me to do nothing about that, to not look out for you and Jackson?"

But no one asked him to. No one *ever* asks him to, but

always thinks he needs to. He always thinks he needs to bubble me, shelter me.

Last night, I admit I had been weak. But what he needed to do, he did. He was there for me. He listened.

He didn't need to fight my battles.

I turned away, and warm hands came down on my shoulders, pulling me in.

"I don't get why you're mad," he said, hunkering down to my level, holding me. "She probably only wanted money or something. Had to, considering the place she was staying at. It was filthy."

Filthy?

I stepped away, turning, and he lowered his hands.

"What kind of place?" I asked him.

Confusion wrung through his eyes and he shrugged a little. "Just some place. Garbage everywhere. A bunch of people lived there, too. Probably boarders. Why?"

Boarders? Garbage...?

I left him without words.

The door still opened, I pushed through and found my phone where I left it.

Griffin stayed close behind.

"Roxie?"

I was unable to answer him as I was busy, getting my purse off the coat hook and shoving my phone inside. I moved around him, then went out the side door that connected to the garage.

"Roxie? Roxie, slow down what are you—?"

I opened the door of my Mini Cooper, getting inside without words.

Griffin gripped the door before I could close it. "Rox—"

"You shouldn't have gone to see her," I said, my face boiling. All the anger came so quickly, steadfast.

I shook my head. "I didn't want that, and you should have talked to me before you did."

His hand slid down the door. "Maybe I should have. But that doesn't stop the fact that she needed to be talked to. She'd just keep coming if no one—"

"You don't get it," I said, nearly shaking as I looked him. "I don't want her having *anything* to do with us, Griffin. I don't want her near us, near you. I..."

Dampening my lips, I faced the window, trying to put into words what I was feeling, but found myself unable to. Maybe it was my body, my condition making things a mix in my head and leaving me ineloquent.

I just knew what he was trying to do for me was the opposite of the solution. He thought he was protecting me, making things better, but by talking to Cassidy, going to one of the people that left me so damage in the past, he only hurt me. I didn't want Cassidy having anything to do with me.

But I wanted to protect him from her even more, her and her family's cancer.

I breathed. "Please let go. I need to go out."

In silence, he stood above me. He removed his hand from the door, but only put it above on the roof of my car.

He let out a long breath. "Where will you go?"

I closed my eyes.

"I have an errand to run," I said, facing him. "And I don't need you to do it for me this time."

The words ran deep over his eyes, far into the heart of his blue irises. He wasn't okay with that, what I said, but I doubt he'd try to stop me.

I was proven right when he lifted his hands from the top of my car, stepping back. I closed my door. After starting it, I put the gear into drive, then let off the brake.

Backing away, I left the garage and down the driveway. I

didn't look for Griffin at all until I made it to the street. I couldn't help it.

He had followed me down the driveway with his hands laced behind his neck, and I knew I would never forget the look I saw on his face through my rearview mirror.

He sported the same worry I felt when I woke up to him missing.

Twelve

ROXIE

I TURNED OFF MY GPS, closing out the address Stevie gave me. She'd forwarded it to me after my ex-step-sister left, said Cassidy gave it to her.

Sitting in my car, everything in my stomach pushed up into my throat. Swallowing, I attempted to force nausea down, but the feeling continued to swell. It swarmed my body, sharp with its hit, and I held my stomach.

Why am I here? Why had I come?

I opened my eyes, seeing the scene before me. It was like Griffin said, and so much worse.

Cassidy lived in an underbelly, a place of poverty and chaos. Folks argued in the street, audible even louder from their homes. A couple of people eyed the street down, a clear drug exchange only feet away from me on the sidewalk. And the smell...

It made me gag.

Sanitation wasn't on the up, and I couldn't believe the disarray of the place. I couldn't believe... *she* lived there.

Shaking my head, I didn't understand. I didn't understand so many things. Why was she here? In this city, *my* city, and living this way. She and my other former step-sister... She and Radha had an inheritance, albeit a small one, but I knew of its existence. My dad and his successes were equal to my ex-step-mom, Julie. They had some old money, family businesses in their family and what have you. Cassidy and Radha weren't rich, but they were taken care of, and not...

I eyed the environment. They weren't this.

My head lowered, questioning why again I had come, questioning what she said at my office. She told Stevie she needed to see me, sounding *urgent* to see me. Had Griffin been right? Was it money?

With the state of this place...

"Call," I said, opening my mouth to the air. In the distance, I heard the car telephone feature warm up, then an electronic voice spoke back to me.

"Call," it said, repeating me.

I watched the house, voices spilling out, more arguments.

I parted my lips again.

"Call dad," I commanded, and then the phone rang.

He picked up after the second ring.

"Roxie?"

His voice sounded into the cab of my car, booming a little as I wasn't expecting it.

I rubbed my hand on the steering wheel's leather. "Hey, Dad."

I was currently in contact with my dad and had been for a while. We had a lot to work through over the years, a lot to work *towards*, but together we had made ground. *I* made ground with him, and though, I called him it wasn't often, which was why he probably asked what he did next.

"Is everything all right?"

Squeezing my eyes, I shook my head as if he could see. "Dad..."

"Roxanne," sounded into the car, his voice direct then

followed a breath. "Why do you sound upset? What's wrong, sweet pea?"

He called me that sometimes, always surprising me with it. It brought me back to a place, reminded me of him and good times of my youth. We did have them. I cherished them as they'd been limited due to the situation we'd both found ourselves in with my mom. He'd faded from her toward the end before she took her life and because of that, I'd faded from him.

"Dad, I..." I *hated* calling him like this. I hated being weak. "Dad, Cassidy is here. She's here in Miami."

The words whispered from my throat, and his sigh had my heart jolting, radiating deep in my chest. It was a sigh of expectancy.

It was a sigh of knowing.

"You know," I said, speaking out into space.

He knew, and he didn't tell me?

"I didn't know she'd go to you," he said, breathing. "But that makes sense, I suppose. I turned her away."

Sitting up, I maneuvered against the back of my seat. A bump tapped the wall of my stomach, and I moved my hand over my belly in small circles.

It's okay. Mommy is okay.

It was like Jackson knew sometimes. He always made me aware of him when I was having an off day like my reminder of everything good in my life, himself and Griffin.

"What did she want?" I asked my dad, getting Jackson calm.

He breathed again. "Honestly, I don't know. We didn't get that far. She called me not long ago saying she needed help. I hadn't heard from her since the divorce."

The divorce. I hadn't been around for that. I was in the heart of my freshman year of college, but I could have foreseen separation. My stepmom could be cruel sometimes, passive aggressive in the way she condescended. My dad just didn't see it until I left. She saved it for me under his nose.

"I asked her about her mother Julie and why she was calling me instead of her," he went on. "She couldn't tell me. She just said she needed help. She needed me to help her."

"How did you respond?" I asked, swallowing.

"Roxanne, I've..." he started, but then he stopped. He stopped for so long, and I didn't know if he would finish, but suddenly, he did.

"I couldn't help someone," he started, pausing a moment. "I couldn't help someone who I knew had caused you pain. I love Cassidy. I love Radha."

Radha. I shook my head, not wanting to think about her. She'd been the worst of the two, the cruelest.

"And I still consider them my children, but sometimes..." his voice lowered again. "Sometimes people have to answer to the things they've done. I could not help her. Whatever it was I couldn't. I just couldn't."

He was looking out for me. He was protecting me, too, like Griffin.

"Do you know she's pregnant?" I asked. Because I did. There was no way that detail could be forgotten—the look in a mother's eyes as she held her unborn child.

This made my dad sigh again. "I didn't, but that wouldn't have changed anything."

I closed my eyes.

"Roxie, I want you to stay away from her," he said. "Julie, she can be manipulative, and I'm sure I don't know Cassidy like I used to. I knew her in her youth. I didn't get to know her as an adult. I'm sure the apple doesn't fall far."

But Cassidy had never been that way. She'd never been cruel.

She wasn't until she was.

My gaze moved to her building then, the place she was

staying at. This was the closest I'd been to her in so long outside of the office, and we had been close, so close.

My hand on the wheel, I went to let my dad go.

I was going to leave. I was going to, like he said, but something stopped me.

Someone stopped me.

Cassidy had a sack in her hands, a white one, plastic and sagging with some kind of goods. Maybe it was groceries. Maybe it was something else, but it became irrelevant.

It slipped from her fingers, pooling on the concrete by her plastic sandals, and her hair, so dark, wrapped around her face in the wisps of the wind.

She pulled it away, and when she did, she lifted her head. That's when her lips parted.

Because she stared at me maybe twenty feet away from her.

"Sweet pea?"

I blinked, the gamut of millions of emotions widespread within me.

"I..." my hand braced the wheel, my head shaking. I started the car, and that made something happen.

It made Cassidy move.

She took a step and only one, but it's what her mouth did that made me stop. Her lips mouthed a sound. It mouthed *my* name as she lifted her hand.

"I'm going to let you go, Dad," I said swallowing, and from someplace far away, I heard him say my name. A phrase followed, and it was something I needed. I had heard him say it before, but he was cautious about it whenever he said it. He was cautious about revealing it, his love.

My hands shaking, I had been cautious about revealing it, too. It was something we both had to work through, but whenever it was said it was genuine.

"I love you, too, Dad," I told him because I did, and not just because I needed him. I told him because I loved him.

"Call me if you need me," he responded, a clear smile in his voice. It always sounded when the words were said, and he never expected them. Especially, since in the beginning, he didn't get a response. He waited for it. He waited patiently.

We hung up with each other, the car cutting us off by my command, and I watched a woman who was only a few steps away. She picked up her sack, and I believed right away she'd be over, but for some reason, she didn't. Her head simply dipped, holding her sack to her chest.

Suddenly, she rushed away, and I watched, her sandals taking her toward the rundown building I assumed she lived in.

But she didn't go in. She simply sat outside. There was a bench there, one wide enough for two. She was waiting. She was letting me go to her.

My key fob, the key still inside the engine, I wrestled with. Did I come here actually expecting to talk to her? Did I intend to *do* something today like I insinuated to Griffin?

I studied her again. She wasn't looking at me, the bag in her hands her fascination, as she played with the plastic handle. She very much looked like a small animal, submissive as she bowed to her environment.

I shut the car off, and the door dinged when I opened it. My foot hit the street below. Pocking my keys, I closed the car door, and then I came around. I came to her.

Her head lifted a little, her gaze moving and flicking. Sometimes it was on me sometimes it wasn't. It was like she was too scared to keep it. She never looked at me that way before. In fact, this very much felt like a role reversal. She'd always been the one to make me look up, stand tall.

She'd always had the confidence.

I got right in front of her, a sudden chill moving from the very tips of my fingers to my toes. I covered my arms, not knowing what to say.

It turned out she was the one to make contact.

"Hey," she said, pushing another one of those wild strands behind her ear.

I didn't say *hi* to her. I think because that made it real, this moment real. But I did take a seat. Like I said there was room. It was near her, but not too close.

Slowly, I lowered to it.

Her hand went inside her bag.

"Apple juice?" she asked, pulling out the very thing. It was a six-pack, those cardboard box-things I used to carry in my lunch sack in school.

She shrugged a little. "They were on sale. I don't normally drink them."

She didn't need to explain herself, but she did need to explain why she was there and why she came to find me.

I chewed my lip, my eyes on her. I wouldn't look away.

Her offer untaken, she revoked it, placing the juice boxes back into the bag.

Her head lifted. "How are you?"

My shoulders moved a little. I found I really couldn't do anything else, but for some reason, that didn't put her off. In fact, she did something so familiar it made my insides tear. It made them burn when she smiled at me.

Her head titled with it.

"You look so different," she said, nodding a little. "You look good."

Again, what a role reversal, me the one looking so well. She seemed so frail, weak. I braced my arms again, another chill.

"Roxie," she went on, this conversation so one-sided. Her eyes closed a little, pinching tight. She opened them. "Say something."

And so I did.

"What do you want?" came from my throat. It ached from

my throat. It felt like such a loaded question, coming from a place of history.

It also came from a place of torture. She'd put me through a lot, she and Radha.

She cringed. "Roxie, I know this is a lot, my being here." Her head shook a little. "But I wouldn't have come if I didn't need it. I promise you that."

I was sure she was right about that, for how could someone have the audacity after what she put me through? My childhood had been one of an intense heartache, my sisters what should have been my reprieve. Instead, they had been my agony, my tragedy.

"How did you find me?" pushed from my lips, my nails biting into my arms.

She answered quickly.

"The TV," she said, swallowing, and a shine coated her eyes. She rubbed them. "When you accepted that award, I saw you. I saw what you made. I saw..."

Slow tears blinked from her eyes and down to her dress. She touched them, wiping them away.

"I saw what you *should* have gotten," she went on, her her lips quivering. "I saw what you deserved because you do, Roxie. You deserve every bit of the success, of the world's appreciation and love."

And what, did she want that? Did she want to *take* that, too, what I'd managed to take back for myself?

"And he seems amazing," she said, sniffing. "Griffin."

His name coming from her mouth shot a red haze over me, my teeth coming down over my lip.

My nostrils flared. "You stay away from him. You... You stay away from *us*. You had no right coming here. You have no right being here. You—"

"You're right," she said, coming to stand. She stood because I did.

She lifted her hands. "You're right."

"And you're *damn* right." I came forward. I came to her. "Don't you think you've done enough? Don't you think that *I've* had enough? I finally can live my life without you. Without reminders of you and the mental burden I *still* have to fight through."

Because I did. I did. One doesn't easily come back from a childhood of ridicule. A girl couldn't easily come back from such pain, at least, not me.

I pointed at her. "You and Radha put me through *hell*."

Her hands lowered as she pulled her lip in. "We were children, Roxie."

Laughable. That's all this was.

I placed my hand on my chest. "And what was I, Cassidy? What was I when you rallied your friends against me? When you threw *food* at me and called me shit? You called me those things knowing, *knowing* it would shred me. You know how my mom died."

Her head dipped, no doubt with the memories. They were ones I'd never forget, so why should I let her? She'd known all about my mom. I told her.

My mom's life ended in a battle with her weight, her mental struggles the taker. When she took her life, it sent me to a dark place, one I'd been able to come out of with the support of my new family. My dad had married so quickly, but it had been so good at first. It had been so good before things changed and before life changed us. Because when it was just the three of us, Radha, Cassidy, and me before friends and gossip and the bullshit of girls, it had been so good.

"I was young," Cassidy went on, pushing tears from underneath her eyes. "I was young. I was stupid, and I wanted friends, and when you're that age..."

Her gaze averted, finding her feet. She lifted her head. "It's no excuse, I know, but it's the truth."

My eyes coated and I watched her come forward.

"And it killed me every day, Roxie. To hurt you. In fact, I numbed myself. I numbed myself, so it wouldn't hurt anymore."

The thing was, I numbed myself, too, but I didn't have friends to hide behind. I only had myself.

I can't do this...

Shaking my keys, I turned. I turned, and she followed me.

"I'm going to lose my baby, Roxie."

I froze, the tears leaking, streaming down my face. From behind, I made out steps coming closer, and a hand touched my back.

I turned with it, eyeing the beholder, and though she looked at me, too, she had only one free hand. The other was on her stomach, that little nub.

Tears blinked down a pretty face before me. Even with how messed up she looked, tired. She was still beautiful, always would be.

"I'm going to lose my baby, and I don't know what to do."

My lips moved. "What are you talking about?"

Her hands moved over that bundle, squeezing. "The baby's father, we didn't work out. We're divorced, but it was messy. I called for it, and he wasn't accepting of it. And now... Now, he wants our child, Roxie. He wants to take the baby away from me, limit my rights. He's got money, and he can do it. So much money."

I didn't understand, but then she went on.

"And I have nothing," she said, swallowing. "I don't have a penny. He'll win."

I took a step back. "I don't understand what you want."

Her body shook then, intense and quaking. "The TV said you were a lawyer."

A lawyer. She wanted me to help her. She wanted me to *fight* for her. How ironic, when she never fought for me?

I moved away. "Don't bullshit me. You have money and can afford a lawyer."

"I don't have anything. Curtis, he…" she paused, those tears moving down her face again. "He's smart. He is a businessman, and he took everything from me. I had no protection, my whole inheritance gone. He got everything in the divorce."

Lifting my hands, I covered my arms again, listening.

She breathed. "And I can't get help from my mom. She never thought I should have gotten divorced in the first place. She didn't support it, and has cut me out of her life ever since. And Radha… Radha only supports her decision."

I shouldn't have been surprised, my former stepmom *and* step-sister real pieces of work…

But the twos cruelty had always been toward Cassidy and me… Cassidy was their own flesh and blood.

I guess some things never change.

"Please," Cassidy went on. "I need your help. I would never have asked if I didn't. I don't know where else to go."

From a distance, sirens filled my ears, voices from afar. They came from the rank that surrounded me, the environment I knew my former step-sister was legitimately a part of.

I messed with my keys. "I'm not that kind of a lawyer."

I specialized in business law, but even if I didn't…

"But you have contacts?" she asked, coming forward. "Friends?"

Something in her pleading must have gotten to her because her hand went to her mouth.

Turning, she let more tears fall and I had never seen her like this. She'd always been the strong one. She'd always been the confident one, but now, she was here. Her life had taken her here, and mine had taken me somewhere else.

How the world can change so much in such a small amount of time.

Silence fell between us, only Cassidy, my ex-step-sister, and her tears, and suddenly, she walked away, leaving me.

"I'm so sorry," she said, turning slightly. Bending over, she grabbed her bag, the one I knew to be filled with apple juice cartons.

"This was dumb," she went on, rising. "I was dumb for asking you, for thinking I could ask you, and I'm sorry, Roxie. I'm so sorry."

She brought the bag to her chest, rushing away, and I watched. I watched a broken woman hurry into a rundown house.

I watched who used to be my closest friend, once upon a time, walk away.

Thirteen

GRIFFIN

I SPENT a lot of time thinking after Roxie left, the sun setting around me. I often came out here and did that sometimes, the peaceful waves and sounds of the beach good for my thoughts.

Lost in them, I sat so long that the sun did set, the soft glow of our property lights the only thing to see by. I set them to come on after day reached a certain hour, nothing but a soft hum of light in the air on the beach.

I drew my arms over the tops of my knees, my feet firmly in the sand as I literally *forced* myself not to worry, worry about her and the situation in which she left.

Roxie had been so mad at me, and honestly, I *still* didn't understand the anger. Call a guy dense, but she couldn't expect me not to do something and help her in whatever way I could. I would help at the basic levels, as her husband, but I wasn't just that, and she wasn't just that to me either.

We were each other's best friends.

"I don't want her having anything to do with us, Griffin. I don't want her near us, near you."

She said she didn't want Cassidy near us and I understood

that. The fact had been the very reason *why* I did what I had, to protect our family.

My gaze searching the beach, I caught my phone in the sand near my feet, the screen still unlit with a call, or even a text from my wife. Just sitting here was damn foolish and I picked it up, unable to take the waiting anymore.

After dialing, I took the device to my ear and had no regrets. I'd given Roxie her time, her space, and now...

The glass door behind me sliding open got my attention. As I turned around, my gaze traveled back to the house, my position on the beach just behind it. We had a fence separating our backyard from the beach, and I sat there, watching while my wife approach me.

Roxie was here as if she never left and I returned my phone to my side, going to stand up. But when she raised her hands, I stayed in my position, letting her come to me. The bell of her dress swayed in the light wind with her strides, and everything flooded back upon seeing her, those feelings of wanting to keep her close, safe. Arriving, Roxie lowered to the beach, but I had to have her in my arms, taking her and our child close to me.

She came without resistance, snuggling close, and I hadn't realized how anxious I'd been sitting here. My thoughts had taken the path of worst case scenario in the last few hours, her whereabouts unknown.

Bringing my arm around her, around them both, I still couldn't rest easy even though she'd returned. There was so much between us, her last words between us.

"I'm so mad at you," she whispered, pushing her small arms around me, as well as she could with her belly. She said what she had, but even with her words, she held me tight. That hold had been both of us, equally.

Drawing my hand down her arm, her heat, I let her words

flow over me. I did know she was mad. She'd told me that before she left.

"I know," I said, closing both arms around her.

Her body moved with her sigh, and I wanted to ask her why she was mad, as well as where she went and why she felt she needed to leave instead of talking to me.

I chose to ease into all of it, deciding to tell her why I did what I had first.

"But when it comes to you, Roxie," I said, "our family, you can't expect me not to act, to *not* be there for you in any way I can."

And she had to know that, and because of the way I felt, I couldn't apologize, not for wanting to take care of her. I'd always take care of her. Perhaps, she knew that because she didn't say anything.

"Where did you go?" I asked. I did want to give her space, but when it came to this topic, her safety...

Dark lashes opened toward the beach, the waves.

"I had to see what she wanted," she said, and I fought my first reaction and what I knew would be frustration in my voice, my words.

Squeezing Roxie's arm, I stayed silent.

Though, only at first.

"I'm sorry, baby. But I'm not really okay with that," I told her being honest. "I confronted her so you wouldn't have to."

Warm fingers touched my jaw, reaching up. She shifted in my arms and stared at me with eyes that made me want to hold her tight, keep her forever and never let go. She was that beautiful, that special, my wife.

She pressed her forehead to mine, smelling warm. Like sugar.

"So you see why I'm mad now? Mad that you went?"

Lifting my head, I stared at her now, confused.

She breathed. "Your impulse to see her, shield me from her, is the same reason why I went today."

"Roxie—"

"To shield you from them," she said, her fingers bumping over the rough surface of my jaw. I hadn't shaved yet, my mind already too consumed.

Her thumb touched my mouth. "My old stepfamily, my step mom and sisters are *poison*, Griffin. They hurt me in ways, affected me in ways..."

Her hand was shaking now, her body tense. I gripped her fingers and her gaze escaped.

"I can't have them anywhere near you," she said, closing her eyes. "I can't. I'm not strong enough. They're cruel and terrible, and I won't have them near you. It hurts. I—"

"Okay. All right," I said, pulling her into my arms. Her back to my chest, she stayed there, rested there, and as we both went silent, out breaths in the night the only sounds between us, I finally did get it. Her anger from before and why she had it.

She wanted to protect me, keep me from the people who'd brought her pain. I understood because I'd been trying to do the same thing for her.

We always did protect each other, didn't we?

I brushed my lips against her brow, viewing out into the crashing waves on the beautiful beach we owned. We had neighbors, but this section was ours, legal and binding.

She fell into my arms, eyes shutting to the wind, and as she did, I finally felt peace. All we had needed to do was talk to each other, get on the same page.

I pushed my hands down her arms.

"Did you do what you needed to do?" I asked after a while. I wanted to hear it. I wanted her to tell me, to listen to her.

She nodded, her eyes opening. Suddenly, she sat up in my arms, and I let her turn, face me.

"I need to do something," she said, playing with the sand a little. "And I think going out, seeing her today, made me realize that."

I played with her hair, strands always escaping the messy way she put it up. I was going to listen to her, be the support I think she needed.

But then she said something even *I* hadn't expected.

"I think I need to help her," she said, and my fingers fell from her hair, my shoulders stiffening.

Her lips moved. "I think I need to do it. I think helping her will give me closure."

"I'm sorry. Help her with what?" I asked raising my hand but not my voice. I stayed calm.

It didn't matter if I was feeling the opposite way inside. I think she felt my frustrations, though because she pushed her fingers through her hair.

"She needs a lawyer," she said, dropping her hand. "She's pregnant and going through a messy custody battle post her divorce. She has nothing but her unborn child and that's exactly what he wants. He's fighting for full custody of their unborn child. He wants to take her baby away."

Jesus.

I rubbed my brow, hearing everything she said, and also understanding why she wanted to help. But something I didn't think *she* understood was how she was being used. She was pregnant, and her sister obviously knew that. She pulled at Roxie's sympathy. She was taking advantage of her.

I decided to tread lightly here, the issue more than sensitive.

"I can see why you want to help," I started, nodding. "And this woman, Cassidy, obviously genuinely needs help. But you must see the angle she's playing at, here. Both her and *you* being pregnant? It's very convenient, and she's probably pretty desperate."

"You think she's taking advantage of me."

The words were very much a statement.

I pushed my hand over my hair. "I know she is. She has to be. It's just too convenient. And you're not even that kind of lawyer, Roxie. You can't help her that way."

My wife had such a big heart, but... this was way beyond her wheelhouse even if she wanted to help.

I expected a challenge, to be challenged by what I said. I proposed some good arguments, as to why she *shouldn't* do this.

But getting on her knees, she didn't give that to me. Instead, she placed her hands on the sides of my neck.

"I need your support," she said, touching her forehead to mine. The breeze around us, the beach before us she smelled like heaven, my own kind bottled and branded for me.

"Please," she breathed, and then she kissed me, touching me in the ways that drove me crazy.

My cock pulsed underneath her hand, rock hard with no give thanks to the confines of my jeans.

My hips thrust to meet her palm. "Roxie..."

Her hand slid underneath my t-shirt, shots of heat surging directly into my abdomen. Her lips on mine, I knew exactly what she was doing, her hands on me.

Intercepting, I held her back, catching her as she attempted to go for my jeans. We couldn't just... *sex* our way around it, the problem.

Forcing my body to calm, I held her hand, kissing her palm.

"I do support you, Roxie," I told her. Because I did, so much. I shook my head. "I support everything you do. I love you."

I'd move the heavens and the Earth for this woman, and she had to know that. I would if I physically could.

Breathing, she kissed my hand too, running her lips along my finger.

"I know," she said and the ache in her voice I heard at full volume.

Laying her head on my chest, she said nothing and even though, we were in the most peaceful environment in the world, our home we both created and built upon, I felt something so loud between us. It resonated in the air, crackled audibly despite how much I hated the fact.

She wanted to help this girl. She wanted to help despite what she'd done. I could only gather that was because of what she said.

My wife needed closure, to help someone, not for this woman's sake...but her own.

This, helping Cassidy, was very much for her, no one else. I also knew for a fact my wife was struggling with something, an issue that took her to her counselor once upon a time.

Maybe this would help.

I had no idea what Roxie struggled with. She hadn't told me, but I had a feeling if I challenged her on this, kept her from closing this door with her ex-step-sister, I might not only make the issue she was having worse...

But force some resentment toward me as well.

My sigh rang heavy in the night, but I knew in my heart what I had to do.

What I had to let *her* do.

"If you do this," I started, pulling back to stare in her eyes. They were so wide, passionate, and kind.

As well as hauntingly beautiful.

My thumb tilted her chin up. "If you help Cassidy... Then you have to promise me you'll let this go. It's not good for you,

Roxie. It's not good for our family. You help her this one time, then that has to be it. You have to be done."

Because *I* couldn't handle anything more, she might offer this woman. It may be the most selfish thing in the world, but I couldn't allow my wife amongst someone, in a situation too long that would be detrimental to both her health and the life of our unborn child.

She stared at me for a while after I said that, the waves crashing ahead of us. The night had fallen, but despite the fact I made out her nod.

"If that's what you need," she said, touching her forehead to mine, and she knew me so well. That promise... her faith I needed so much.

As well as something else.

Easing her lips up, I gave her a soft kiss in the night, bracing her cheek as I hummed my need for *her* along her lips. My cock stiffened in a fury, and her thighs jiggled when I bunched her dress above her hips, her breasts bouncing after I shrugged the material over her head and tossed it to the beach. This left her exposed, open to the ocean air, but we'd done this before so many times. Our elderly neighbors never went out after the sun set, so we had our privacy.

But even if they did...

I took her lips, guiding her to slide her perfect body on top of mine, and she was perfect, created for me—mine.

Her belly was swollen, as much her breasts, her skin toasted and warm underneath my hands. Hips wide, full, they were exemplary for my hands, my cock as I drove inside her.

"Griffin..."

I squeezed her breast, easing one of her lace cups off to tease one of her peaks.

My thumb outlined the erect chocolate kiss that was her perfect brown nipple, needing a taste.

I took that taste, and she moaned, cupping the back of my

head, as I sucked. She had her own kind of indescribable taste, hot and sweet; amazing.

My hand on her stomach, I lifted my hips, seeking her heat through her panties. So wet, she left a spot on my jeans.

"Fuck…"

That fell from both our lips, Roxie's hips gyrating as she dry humped me. Reaching, she eased my shirt off, and I figured she wanted to take some of the control here, her hand reaching down to unbuckle my jeans.

She had a smile on her lips while she did it, looking innocent, teasingly so. Her dark hair slid over her cheek, reminding me that she was anything but innocent. She took entirely too long to undo my pants, and by the time she did, my dick sang at the freedom, and equally burned beneath her touch.

She jerked me, two hands, as she worked my cock. Half naked and one breast falling out of her bra, she was the epitome of a wet dream for me.

And with her being pregnant.

I held her tummy, my large hands not even big enough to cradle her.

I moved a hand to her hip, pulling a breath through my teeth, as she pumped me. The tip of the head glistened in the soft lighting of our home's outdoor lights, ready for so much more.

I wanted her on her knees. I wanted her, but she threw me for a loop when she eased back. As she slid her panties away with two fingers, she showed me a dark mound, untampered with, natural, and it took all I had in me not to ease her up to my face and bury my tongue inside her.

I waited, patient while she allowed me into that perfect, warm space.

But once inside.

I groaned, the chore of going slow while consumed by her heat that of an ungodly torture.

"Baby…"

She swiveled her hips, cutting me off, and when she started bouncing…

Fuck.

I took control then, bracing her hips. Holding her tight, taking her along for this ride, I used the force of my thighs to slam into her, fucking her from below.

The pleasure on her face I lived for, I'd *die* for, and I watched her, the most beautiful sight above me.

Pushing my hands along her descended abdomen, I laid my head back to the sand, cruising out this ride, this pleasure I myself had somehow been blessed with. It wasn't supposed to turn out that way for me. Being in sports, a player's lifetime usually consisted of drugs, parties, and women who never even gave a guy anything close to love. They didn't have this. *I* wasn't supposed to have it.

But I did.

I spilled into her, milking her with every thrust and pulling her orgasm out of her. It came quickly, hard, and that pulse, that damn pulse of hers tight around me vibrated well into my thighs.

I slid her off when she was finished, her body weak. To the sand, I gave her my arm to lay on. I'd give her any limb she wanted.

All she had to do was ask.

8th Month of Pregnancy

Fourteen

ROXIE

KNOTS COILED, internal with no give. My stomach clenched tightly, and I couldn't breathe correctly, my fingers going to my necklace.

You can do this. You can.

A lot brought me to this place now, my present and even my past. I wasn't the same girl Cassidy knew back then. I built a life for myself, was having a family.

Pushing my hands over my belly, I closed my eyes.

I was a different person, had different things and tools in my arsenal, and I could use them. I *did* use them every day I came to work and did the things I loved, for the people I felt needed just as much of a chance as I had. I built something, created something I was proud of because I had the strength. And I had the strength to do this, do something for someone without thought or even hope of appreciation. I didn't want Cassidy's sorry. I was way beyond that. I just wanted to know that I could do something for her without any type of thanks.

I very much wanted this for myself.

Looking up, something captured my attention, activity ahead from behind the window and office I sat in. They must have been finished, and that confirmed when into the hall came Kerry Donovan, my friend and as well as a lawyer in another life. She'd retired not long after she married her husband Kendrick, but she came out of retirement for today.

She came out of retirement for me.

I sat in her downtown office, her practice, which was run by herself and her family. Though she didn't frequent the office, they kept a space for her, my friend one of the top attorneys in family law once upon a time. She used that knowledge, helping someone for me.

In the weeks since I came to Kerry initially, she used that time to prepare and today, well, today was the day of the first meeting, my friend acting representation for... Cassidy.

My former step-sister came out of the conference room within my view with who I knew to be Kerry's second chair Edina behind her.

Her hands twisted up, Cassidy walked with her head dipped down. She stood in between Edina and Kerry lacking everything I remembered her having as a child.

She was much like that day I went to where she lived, withdrawn and quiet. Wearing a pale, pink dress and flat shoes without flash or glamor, my ex-step-sister took up little space. She remained small, quiet and had since the moment she arrived into Kerry's office. I watched her the moment she came in, quiet myself in the space Kerry made for me in her office. I kept a close eye, feeling it necessary. I may have chosen to help Cassidy, but I'd be watching out for my friend as well. A top attorney or not, I made my friend susceptible to her. This was on me if Cassidy took advantage. None of this would go down unless I was present.

I turned, moving on the couch cushion. Kerry had clear glass so I could see quite well across the office, the women moving amongst the other employees and busy attorneys bustling by. Through the pack of it all, I could see the ladies well. Kerry had her hand behind Cassidy, guiding her out.

But the women weren't coming out of that room alone.

A man came out directly after them, tall with well-oiled hair. He'd been quick to smile when he came in, but it had always been a short-lived expression. Like he did it only out of politeness or formality. He made his handshakes short, too. He gave one to Kerry, then her second chair Edina, nodding at Cassidy only briefly before his client joined the party, the final member of the procession line.

He turned heads like he'd done when he came in, Cassidy's ex-husband. Skin deep with color and hair of a dark, even tone, Cassidy's ex was everything I imagined someone like her would be with. He was equally beautiful to her, stunning from his expensive-looking suit to well-polished shoes.

His eyes revealed something else, though. They were still beautiful just like the rest of him, but the way he used them made me see past the surface. I think it was the way he watched Cassidy, slick and even borderline leering. The entire gaze made Cassidy's body tight and her eye contact shifted away, her hands wrestling beneath herself.

But that didn't stop her ex's pursuit.

He actually stepped forward, attempting to say something to her.

Too bad my friend got there first.

Kerry was quite polite about it, professional, but she wasn't having him talking to her client without permission.

She stepped slightly in front of Cassidy and through the spaces of the passing people in her office, I noticed her smile, a few words passing from her lips. I had no idea what they were, but whatever they consisted of broke the illusion for only a moment, that beauty of a man who sported such perfection a moment ago.

A cruelty hit his eyes then, making them narrow, and for a

second, the expression shocked me still. That was how powerful it had been, tense.

With a shift of his shoes, the man stepped away, his lawyer in tow. Kerry only watched him for a second before turning to her own client. She spoke a few words to Cassidy and whatever they'd been made Cassidy's head lift. She nodded, shaking Cassidy's hand before releasing her to Edina. Her second chair escorted Cassidy away and my friend headed in the direction of her office.

Turning around, I took a few short breaths, my heart racing for some reason. I'd been fine before, and I would be fine now. All of this would be over soon. I had friends behind me, and soon, things would go back to the way they were. Cassidy would be out of my life again and I... I'd have closure.

Kerry Donavon quite literally brightened up a room when she came in, so glamorous in even the plain brown suit of an attorney. Her black pumps with red bottoms clicked the floor when she entered, and I was graced with the kindest smile, my dear friend always good for one of those.

Forcing bravery into my limbs, I made myself stand. I wanted to know how everything went in there if everything was okay.

"How'd it go?" I asked her, the confidence I knew I held. What I was doing was the right thing. It had to be.

Coming further into her office, Kerry placed a file on her desk. That smile remained on her face, but I couldn't help noticing the tightness of it.

She sat back against her desk.

"It's a rough situation, Roxie," she said, sighing. She shook her head, the length of her haircut modest, but always pristine. "That woman's ex-husband is a character. Did you know, he's a mob affiliate?"

I had no idea. In fact, the very notion shocked me.

How could she end up with someone like that?

"Though he hides it under the guise of legitimate business practices," she went on. "He's hard, *tough*. He wants Cassidy's child, and he just might get what he's after. The courts usually favor the mother, but not when they have nothing. And she doesn't have anything, Roxie. Her inheritance was significant, but she didn't think to get protection. He took it all in the divorce."

I didn't know how I felt about that, turning away. This didn't sound like Cassidy—she was always so smart. She had always been I thought... better. She was better than this no matter how things went down between us.

She was beautiful, confident, and top of her class. Cassidy had always been someone I aspired to be, even when she was hurting me.

Lifting my head, I could still see her. Edina had given her a seat in the foyer, Cassidy's head down with her hands in her lap.

What had happened to her? Was it that guy or...

I didn't know. I just knew the woman out there wasn't the one I knew. Something had happened to her. Something had changed.

"I feel bad for her," Kerry chimed in, coming to my side. She watched Cassidy as I was, my friend, shaking her head. "He's a real piece of work and wouldn't even let her get a word in edgewise. I had to intercede several times."

"What can you do for her?" I asked.

I think I needed that. I needed that for her and for myself. When I originally went to see my former step-sister, I had no idea why. It had been on impulse, sheer curiosity driven by pain. But at some point, it became something else, and I think I realized that after I spoke to her. Something made me fight to help her and that same something even made me challenge the man I loved.

It wasn't a mystery to me Griffin didn't want me to help

Cassidy, and his objection was the same reason he went out to her in the first place. He wanted to fix this, fix it for me. But I didn't need him to fix it. I needed him to step back and let me get a handle on this myself. That was the only way *I'd* be at peace, my heart at peace.

I needed to know I had the strength to overcome Cassidy and our history together. This woman had been my world once upon a time. I went to sleep by her taunts, and though she hadn't been the fire starter like her sister Radha, she did nothing to stop the flame. She was there for all of it, every word, every chant. She had been my misery, yes, but she would no longer be my pain.

And that was a promise I made to myself.

Kerry and I both watched the woman outside her office. Edina had returned to Cassidy, a cup of coffee in her hand for the woman.

"I'll make it so she keeps her child," Kerry said, answering my question. Then her hand lifted, waving through the glass with one of her kind smiles.

Facing forward, I noticed who she waved at, Cassidy, her coffee cup in hand.

I froze, standing there without reaction. Before, the distance had been so far between us, and the busy people in Kerry's office concealed my gaze, but there was none of that anymore. There was Cassidy and there was me—the two of us without distraction.

I didn't know how to react. Much like that day at my office, I was left without words or thought. Cassidy, on the other hand, made no effort not to react.

She made no effort, not to thank me.

She lifted her hand, but she didn't do so to Kerry who stood beside me. She lifted her hand to me. I know because she mouthed something, three words: "Thank you, Roxie."

Her back faced me after that, still no reaction from me.

Edina escorted her out, and Kerry turned, pressing a finger to her intercom.

"Yes, Ms. Donavon," a voice sounded from the room. I assumed her receptionist.

Kerry bent over the speaker. "Can you put Ms. Davis into a car?" she asked referring to Cassidy. "She lives in South Ridge."

"Of course, Ms. Donavon, right away."

"Join me for lunch," Kerry said to me, rising up. She went behind her desk, picking up her purse.

A wide smile highlighted her brown eyes. "We could go to that quaint little sandwich shop down the street. Take a load off."

Thoughts of Cassidy lingering fresh in my mind, I blinked, nearly missing what my friend said.

"Sandwich shop?"

Kerry nodded. "Mmhmm. My staff and I used to go all the time when I was at the office."

"Sure, yeah. That's fine."

After taking a few moments, I got my purse, using the couch to steady myself when I bent to pick it up off the floor. I placed it next to the couch but struggled a little on my way back up, all this belly throwing off my equilibrium a bit.

A hand came to my arm.

"Aren't you just the cutest little pregnant woman?" my friend said, laughing when she helped to stabilize me.

"I'm glad someone thinks so," I told her smiling a little. "I feel huge, my feet swollen."

"It all comes with the territory. Come on. We'll get you in a car soon, so you don't have to walk anymore."

I nodded at her, ready to go when she was. Kerry opened the door to her office. I followed her but hesitated when someone else re-entered the room directly in front of me, the foyer outside of Kerry's office.

Cassidy didn't notice me, her head down, has been her M.O. since she came back into my life. Her lidded coffee cup still in hand, she headed back over to the seat she'd been at. She must have forgotten something because when she bent, reaching next to the chair, she came back with a lightly-colored sweater in her hands.

But that wasn't the only thing I observed.

She had a bandage under her arm, easily concealed when she rested it by her side. I guess that's why I hadn't noticed it before.

By this time, Edina had come back into the room. She placed her hand behind Cassidy, smiling as she guided her out again.

"Roxie?"

I walked past Kerry at her door, following Cassidy until she fell out of my sight. She entered an elevator, amongst many when she pushed onto it in the busy office building.

"Roxie? What's wrong, honey?"

I blinked, my view cut off from Cassidy as the elevator doors closed.

"Did you see that bandage?" I asked Kerry, still in wonder of it. I didn't remember that the day I saw her at her house.

Had she had that before?

I wondered if she had and if so when she'd gotten it.

As well as how.

My friend coming in beside me put me off by her expression. Kerry loved to smile. That was just her way. But she wasn't smiling anymore.

Not at all.

She put her hand on my arm. "Roxie... knowing what happened will just sit heavy on your heart. It did mine, which was why I advised a shelter for her. She seems to have too much pride though for that."

"A shelter? What? Why would she need to go there?"

Her hand moved down my arm. "Because she got that wound at that place she currently lives at. Someone cut her."

Cut her...

My hand smoothed over my belly, a little wonder inside, one not unlike Cassidy's. I was further along, but she had one, too. She had a baby, too.

I swallowed. "What do you mean she was cut? What happened?"

"I just know there was an altercation. She got in the wrong person's way. Those things happen."

"She's pregnant, Kerry."

"I know, sweetie. Which is why I said knowing what happened will just sit heavy on your heart. You can't do anything for her, and she won't stay at a shelter. My hands are tied."

Her hands are tied.

"We'll win for her," Kerry said, coming around me. She took my hands. "That will get her out. The finalizing of her case will come with a healthy child support settlement. She and the baby will be well taken care of. I'm making sure of that, fighting for her."

She was right, winning would get Cassidy out, out this situation and whatever mess she'd gotten herself into. But my dear friend, as amazing as she was had been wrong about something, too. The information may have sat heavy on my heart.

But I wasn't without the means to do something for my ex-step-sister.

Fifteen

GRIFFIN

The production schedule will be 6-9 months, as well as time scheduled for reshoots. The production schedule will begin...

The contract curled in my hands, affecting me deep in my gut. Call a guy simple, but movies taking this much time to make quite epically, blew my mind. I hadn't anticipated spending this much time away from Roxie, the baby too after he was born...

This really is impossible, is it?

That knocked the wind out of my sails a little, the knowledge of that. I started to get a little excited about it all, the talk of it all...

Roddy Price's movie offer floated over my head like a dark cloud since the day of the offer, when in the beginning it had been such an opportunity.

That'd been the day so much drama came into our lives, Roxie's former sister coming out of nowhere. My wife was handling all of that now, closing the door to a bunch of stuff that had no business flurrying around us. I wasn't happy with the ultimate decision she made, but as this seemed to be a temporary situation, a *temporary* inconvenience, I let the issue go at the moment. From what my wife told me, her friend Kerry would be handling most of the situation, her former step-sister's actual attorney in all this, while Roxie waited on the sidelines. There shouldn't be really *any* interaction between the two of them, and that set my heart at ease a little. We'd be waiting while Kerry handled all this and then my wife could let go. We could move on.

I thought the next step might have been the contract in my hands. I had no idea how I'd make this work, with my wife's busy schedule and of course mine. Adding a newborn to the mix was just another level in regards to the complications that would keep me from going away for months at a time to shoot a movie, but I thought maybe, just maybe we'd have a miracle. I could fly in and out. I could make it work. But it was just too much time, too much...

Roxie and the baby would just need me too much. This wasn't how things were with my basketball schedule, where I could cut events and swap out opportunities for my job with those of my family obligations. It had been a juggling act over the years, but I *always* managed to make it work come hell or high water.

But this is just too much...

The contract felt heavy in my hands, my agent reminding of it this morning. I hadn't even gotten a chance to tell Roxie about the opportunity yet, too much going on and with the odds of me not even taking it, I didn't see the point in telling her.

Putting the contract down, I stared out the window, my travels taking me above the clouds today. I was headed home to Texas for a few hours and was always glad for them.

I had these check-ins with my pop more and more these days and what was now known to be the family business, all three of my brothers involved in something my pop started once upon a time. We all had our hands in *Chandler & Sons*

Furniture Co. and what a business it had become over the years.

The beginnings had all been my pop, a hardworking man who started in construction himself. After years of back-breaking work, he decided to start his own business, and I had been happy to be one of the early benefactors. That commitment went on well after the loan was paid, though. This business was just as much mine as anyone else who had a direct role in the business' foundation, and I was proud to say I had my hands in the company quite a bit.

I liked it that way, being involved. Not because I was anal-retentive or anything, but because I truly liked working with my family. I really did see myself doing something like this in the future, being a businessman or something. That only helped that I got to do so with some of the people I cared about the most.

My pop was in charge, but the rest of my brothers were well in deep and just as committed as our pop was. My oldest brother Hayden held some of the management roles at the place and my brother Brody, well, he did deliveries along with his fiancée, Alexa, or I guess Alex for short. He met this girl out of the blue one day, and she rightly changed his life. The two had been inseparable since she managed to work her way into his heart and were expecting a child, too. Though, not as far along as Roxie. Perhaps, that had been the sign my brother needed to finally stop making his woman sweat and pop the question to her. But my brother and his committing definitely hadn't been the reason for the proposal layoff. The two had been living like they were married for years along with two members of her family, her nephew, Aiden and sister Elena. Honestly, getting married was something my brother probably just hadn't slowed down enough to think about. He and Alex kept busy, her just as much involved in my family business as the rest of us.

As excited as I was to see my family today, check-in, I had all this contract stuff sitting on my shoulders. I just had to tell Deanna no, and that was that. I had no time for the commitment.

No matter how truly awesome it did sound.

The wheels of the plane hitting the tarmac brought me back into reality. Deanna had set the flight up, as well as the private car waiting for me when I got out. I really hated being chauffeured around my old stomping grounds, but it made sense, as I wasn't in town often enough to justify keeping my own ride here. I got inside the car and then sat back, letting my driver do his job.

My pop's furniture shop resided deep in the country, a truly awesome backdrop of rolling hills and scenic landscapes behind it. I had lived here a big chunk of my life, in Texas, and as much as I loved the beautiful home and life I'd made for myself and my family, nothing took a guy's breath away better than being back where he grew up. When pop debated where he'd put his business there hadn't really been one, a debate that is. This was home. *Here* was where it needed to be, and the rest of my family had been completely on board with him.

My driver pulled up in front of a modest-sized warehouse, those picturesque hills behind it. My driver got out and went to open the door for me, but I beat him to it. Something about them doing that part of the job made me feel kinda enti-tled. I could get my own door and did, thanking the man with a tip before getting my things together. I pushed the contract into my back pocket, then got out, heading toward the sizable production my pop had going on.

Workers towed everything from rocking chairs to the bare materials it took to make them, and that was just on the outside. Behind those warehouse doors was truly a produc-tion, people sawing away and constructing fine works of art. We had tables, couches, and chairs, and even jungle gyms being made for children to play on, the employees hard at work as they always were. Many of them passed a friendly expression my way, my face only familiar to him. They waved at me, which I quickly returned, then took a moment of appreciation for everything there.

What my pop made for himself was truly amazing. His business outsourced inventory to furniture shops all over the world, greatly expanding the reach of his own local furniture shops. Pop had several, not just the one he originally made when he kicked off the company. This whole thing was my pop's dream and working together as a family, I think was all of ours. I never saw my brothers more than when this whole thing began a few years ago. Even old Colton made his way out there sometimes. He did the branding, an artist, as well as a basketball player.

Grateful for it all, I made the moves to take steps forward. I planned to head toward my pop's office located in the back of the building.

But it seemed I couldn't get there on my own.

Hair chopped off, my brother Hayden was starting to look more and more like an old man and less of the scalawag he used to be back when we were kids. He really had come into his own since working for pop, a man of the business world instead of just a guy working under his father. We all changed in that way in these few short years and how interesting it was to see.

Hayden's hand went out to me. Pulling me in, my brother patted my back and I got to see the man up close.

A wide smile touched his lips.

"The old bum's come to check-in on us, huh?" he asked, shaking me a little before pulling away. Initially, he lobbed off his hair so he could deal with the public, my brother the face of the company. If one wanted an order, they went through him first.

I pushed his arm. "Nice, man."

"What? We just haven't seen you in a while is all."

He only left out my visit three weeks ago and the one not long before that. He was obviously giving me a hard time, as brother's do.

Sliding his arm around my shoulders, he guided me toward the back, giving me the lowdown on the things I liked to hear about, business or otherwise.

He spent the most time on his family.

"I tell ya, Griff, that kid of mine is borderline odd," my brother said, opening the doors of the freight elevator for me. We needed the space considering the size of the stock we hauled around here. We went inside, and he closed the doors, grinning at me.

"Karen and I couldn't even get Sarah to touch her homework when she started school, but Crissy..." He whistled, propping his hands on his hips. "She rips her schoolbag open before we can even get her inside. Her teacher says she's top of her class."

"So what is that exactly?" I asked, taking a moment to open the doors when we reached the warehouse's top level.

I grinned upon exiting.

"High marks in finger paints?" I asked. "She's in daycare still, right?"

From what I understood, an accelerated learning program, but still... daycare.

As expected, I got a nice, strong sock in the arm when he got into the hallway. My brothers and I took turns with Hayden, yanking his chain and what not. This man was the proudest papa one could ever meet when it came to his kids. I guess he learned from the best—we all would eventually when it came time.

He pointed at me. "And the best damn finger paints you

could ever see and don't you forget it. My girl's gifted. Both of them are."

Lifting my hands, I only smiled, lowering my head to the truth of that statement. I had no doubt he was right.

I paid for my teasing in the next moment when my brother's arm went around my neck. He pulled me into a headlock I could probably get out of, my training for ball playing allowed me to surpass the strength of my big brother long ago, but I let him have that one. I always did.

"You'll be doing it, too, soon, string bean," he said, my childhood nickname holding strong despite the lack of truth to it. I hadn't been an actual *string bean* in years.

He hugged my shoulders. "A man couldn't be prouder of his kids come time. They'll sneeze, and you'll want to bake them a cake in congrats."

I hadn't doubted that and I knew before Roxie and I got pregnant that's how it'd be. I couldn't wait to teach Jackson things, grow just as much with him, as he did alongside me.

I must have had those thoughts lingering on my face in that hallway, because my brother stopped, his smile slow as he looked at me.

He rubbed my shoulders. "Where's Roxie, huh? She hasn't been coming with you lately."

My check-ins did usually include Roxie, but like he said, not for a while.

I pushed my hands into my pockets. "She's officially no fly and has been for a little bit, so we're being safe."

I purposely left the part about her former step-sister coming back into our lives out of the conversation. He didn't need to know. Cassidy was a non-issue, and she'd be gone soon. Almost as if she never was.

The white walls took us on to my pop's office, a bit more back and forth between us. Everything was good, as per usual here, but I loved to see it up close and enjoyed seeing my family even more. In the business I was in, it was easy to lose track of my loved ones. But the family business kept us connected, gave me an excuse to come down and just be, be here with them and spend what time I could.

I went to turn the knob of a wide door and see the man who raised me behind it, but to my surprise, I got something else just before.

Hayden's hug was firm, hard and I didn't resist it.

"You tell no one about this," he said, laughing a little, as he held me tight. I could hear the emotion in it.

He pulled away, and I saw it just the same, a little red in my big brother's eyes.

"I always thought you'd be something, Griff, and you are, something so great," he said, shaking his head. He smiled. "But even with all that, you being a dad I'm sure will trump everything you've done so far. I'm proud of you, string bean. We all are. I just thought you should hear it."

I didn't know which one of those statements got me, but something kept me from opening that door to my pop's office right away, as well as hugging my big brother again.

"You tell no one," I said, emotion in my voice.

Nodding, Hayden pulled away, and we solidified our pact with a fist bump.

A whole party was in my pop's office, my pop himself, my stepmom... yeah, I had one of those. My pop married not long after I had. He'd met someone in the hospital, a nurse who cared for him after his heart attack a few years ago. It'd been a trying time for all of us, but his wife, Ann... she made it just a bit easier. He found strength in her, and I bet, if asked, she would have said the same.

I got a nice tight hug from her. The woman reminded me so much of my own woman at home. I think it was her kindness, as well as her loving smile.

The aged, black woman pulled away, and when she did,

she returned to the side of my pop, his arm readily available to welcome her.

The man literally shined light when he was around her, something I hadn't seen much of in the twenty-plus years. My mom left my family so young I barely remembered her. Pictures were all I had left, ones buried unfortunately with the memories. It couldn't be helped. I'd just been so young when she left.

Pop patted Ann's shoulder. "No Roxie with you again today, Griff?"

What could I say, my wife was loved, cherished by everyone, not just me.

Hands in my pockets, I gave them the same words I shared with my older brother. Roxie wasn't here. She wasn't, but she wanted to be. She always would as she was just as much a part of our family, as me.

We all reconvened around my pop's desk, my pop and Ann behind it with Hayden and myself taking a seat in front. I asked about Brody during the gathering, but apparently, he was out on deliveries.

"Hayden, tells me things have been going okay here," I said, sitting back in my chair. That's usually how these check-ins went. I asked about the progress, and we all sat around and talked about it, so imagine my surprise when my pop's big hand rose in the air, waving me off.

"We 'gon hear your news first, boy," he said, crossing his legs behind his desk. "Ann told me a bit, but we need you to fill in the blanks. And be thorough now. You know your grandmama. She's gonna want to know everything."

My gram did want to know everything in my life and hell, my Aunt Robin was damn worse, but regarding *this* bit of information I was supposed to share, I had no idea what my old man was talking about.

My brow lifted.

"Pop?"

"Now, don't be doing that now. Deanna already went and told us everything, so you might, as well—"

"Wait. Deanna?" I questioned, holding up my hands. "What exactly did she tell you?"

The room went silent, all eyes either on me or avoiding me. Hayden's traveled away, hand covering his mouth, and Ann's traveled too. By my pop, she wrestled her hands in her lap, but it was Pop's gaze that held fast, tight and relentless. He clearly wanted to know something, something I had no idea of even the content to share.

It was Ann who spoke first.

"Deanna shared your movie news," she admitted, apparently a bit of shame behind the words considering she all but whispered them. In the next instance, she gave my pop a quick pat on his arm, the only one brave enough to do such a thing to the big man.

"And it was supposed to be a secret, Blake," she said to him, a frown following her words. "We agreed he was going to tell us when he was ready."

"Well, he was taking, too, long," Pop grumbled, but I didn't miss the smile behind his goatee highlighted by the occasional white whisker. This woman made him extremely happy, and that showed all over his face. He glowed.

It was me who was sweating bullets.

"Christ."

I spoke the word under my breath, but I was sure it was all over my face. I hadn't even told Roxie about the opportunity yet, and as it turned out, my entire family already knew.

I was the only one who knew my ultimate decision, though.

I moved my hand over my mouth. "Deanna told you guys?"

"She told Ann," Pop said, pushing back from his computer. "The two exchange recipes or something."

"Yes, we do," Ann went on, bumping my pop's arm. "And it took a lot to get the information out of her, Griffin, so don't be too mad."

Normally, I wouldn't be. I wouldn't because this was an exciting opportunity. This was quite literally the biggest deal of my life, and normally, I *would* be shouting it from the rooftops. I'd want to share it with my family... my wife.

My hands came together. "So, you'll get to go to Hollywood, right?" Ann asked with genuine excitement in her eyes. It lit them up just like my pop when he stared at her. "And your daddy is right. You'll have to tell us everything. And what does Roxie think about all this? She's probably through the moon, right?"

"Of course she is," my pop chimed in, nodding. "The pair of you are always moving mountains together."

"Aren't they, though?" Ann put her hands together. "Such an amazing time for you both."

"And Jackson, too," my pop said. We'd shared the baby's sex and name months ago through Roxie's baby announcement idea, our family forever joyful.

My pop's smile started slow, and when it reached his eyes, I saw his light. But it wasn't toward my step-mom this time.

It was in my direction.

"My blood," he said, that smile higher on the right. "You'll tell us all about it when you go, the people you get to see? And not just for your grandmama. I want to know, too."

He wants to know, too.

"We all do."

Ann's hand smoothed down my pop's arm after her words, nothing but pride in the pairs' eyes, and I couldn't do it. I didn't have the heart to tell them everything, what I'd ultimately decided. I only realized I was staring away when my brother's arm came around my shoulders. He'd done so recently, in the hall before we'd come in.

"I told you we were proud of you," he said, and I realized he knew about the opportunity, too. He had since before we came into the room together.

The entire room went on to ask me more questions, most of which I evaded. How could I let them down?

I wouldn't knock the wind out of their sails, too.

Sixteen

GRIFFIN

I DIDN'T KNOW it was possible to be just as drained from a few hours of conversation as a day on the basketball court, but my family managed to achieve the impossible.

Drained, I dragged myself into the house that night, the plane ride just as tiring as my time spent in Texas.

I just couldn't turn my brain off, my mind wandering. I spent so much time answering questions to offer my family complete honesty. I told them what I knew, and in actuality that had been the easy part. The hard stuff had been the ones that affected my gut, no matter how much I didn't want that.

They asked me how I felt about all of it, the offer and everything.

The sickness only came from the truth.

I was truly honored to get such a role. I wasn't an actor, my chops that of but a few acting classes and some small roles here and there on television. Roddy Price saw out of everyone me, some country hick who one day decided to have a dream. I had no desire to change fields by any means, but this stuff? Well, it was pretty damn cool even for me.

"Roxie?" I called, hanging up my coat, then my messenger

bag. It had the film contract amongst other things involving my family business inside it. I always came home with stuff.

I put my hand on the outside of the bag, that opportunity inside there.

Perhaps, it wouldn't be a big deal to mention the role to her. I had no hopes anything would come of it. I mean, I had already basically decided. But I knew if I was her, and this was the other way around, I'd want to at least hear about it.

Okay, I'll do that.

In any sense, I needed her outside of that. I had a long day and she, no doubt, had much of the same.

All that crap with her former step-sister was a pure mess and hopefully, what she got done while I was away managed to give her a little peace. We could relax tonight, no talk of business, movie roles, or people thrust into our lives that didn't deserve the space. Some of the best times I'd ever had was just us, Roxie and me. We could spend hours just sitting together, lying to together, and now, we had a baby between us to enjoy the time even more.

Sounds like a perfect damn night.

She didn't answer me the first time I called her, so I tried again, making my way through the house. Clanking in the kitchen met my third call, and I rerouted, smiling when I made my way in that direction.

Anytime she spent in there was a good time for her. She enjoyed cooking, the breeze coming off the beach rolling into our kitchen window on her.

Today must have been okay.

I was hopeful, coming around the corner. I expected to see my wife around that corner, *her* hands taking a hot pie out of the oven. But that's not what I saw, *who* I saw.

I saw a stranger, a woman wearing a dress with faded flowers on it and her hair thick over her shoulder in a long braid. She didn't notice me when I came in, and I couldn't see her face as she placed that pie tin down to rest on the kitchen counter.

"Hello?"

I scared her. Hell, her reaction even made me jump.

Her oven mitt covered hand went to her chest and she finally faced me; she had the expression of the purely freaked. Probably because she recognized me.

I sure as hell recognized her.

I took a step forward on instinct. This woman... *that* woman has no business being in my house, and my charge was only halted by the appearance of another.

Roxie's sock-covered feet came to a stop in the kitchen. Her hands on her stomach, on Jackson, she looked just as surprised, as the stranger before us. But the surprise wasn't at seeing the woman.

It was from seeing me.

Roxie

The moment he saw her I *knew* he'd be angry. He met her before, was well aware of her, and I knew her presence in our home he wouldn't like.

But I didn't feel like I had much of choice.

I went to pick up the phone so many times today, *call him* and at least warn him what was to come, but every attempt ended in failure.

My own dismay already filled the space in my head.

I never thought she'd say... yes to help. I never thought... I never thought...

But the fact she had said a lot, the fact Cassidy herself agreed to return home with me instead of going back to the place she lived said so much. It spoke of need, a desperation that most likely went beyond both of us. She had a baby. She was pregnant.

And that's really all there was to it.

I expected a lot from Griffin, frustration, and discord a given. I knew that because I knew him. I could have explained the decision all I wanted, why I needed to continue helping Cassidy and the urgency of it, but that wouldn't matter. He wouldn't understand the decision because of the history between Cassidy and me, and there'd be no way around it. I mean, he'd want to understand. I know he would but simply wouldn't allow himself to. He'd go into protection mode, and that would be it.

It would be this.

"I want her out of my house," he said, not looking at me. He leaned forward, sitting at the end of our bed...

The place he'd escaped barely after I came in the room and tried to explain myself.

The start of a sentence barely left my mouth before he came in here, our room. He was clearly done here.

Griffin dropped his hands between his legs. I hadn't caught his gaze not once since he'd entered the room, my husband staring forward at our bedroom wall.

He moved a hand over his mouth.

"I want her out, Roxie," he continued, his tone firm, final. "I want her out, and that's it. She's out of the house and after that... After that, you leave all this, *her* alone."

He was talking to me like I wasn't capable of making my own decisions. I knew what I was doing, the reality of it, and every interaction, every ounce of my *help* was hard for me.

I breathed.

"She's eating here tonight, Griffin," I said, which he knew because I blurted that out after he stormed in here. Cassidy would be eating here with us tonight before I drove her to a hotel.

She chose to bake for us on her own.

I never approved such a thing. In fact, I hadn't really spoken to her at all since at Kerry's office and even the request to help Cassidy had come from my friend's mouth. It had been *Kerry* who asked if I could lend a hand, *Kerry,* who had pretty much done all the talking until my friend got Cassidy in my car and the pair of us drove off together.

After that had been nothing but silence.

I got Cassidy here, then when it was time made dinner and left her to her own devices.

I explained all this to Griffin. I explained the extent of my help for my former step-sister. I owed her nothing, and I knew that. But I was human as well.

I wasn't heartless.

And I didn't appreciate the ultimatum my husband was giving me here tonight. I realized I told him I'd be helping Cassidy this one time with Kerry's services. But things changed.

This was my house too, and I had a say.

I stepped over to him, taking my seat beside him and could literally feel the hum of his energy coming off him.

I could feel his tension even more.

"There's no harm in helping her this way," I said, firmly. I mean, didn't he know this was hard for me?

This woman had hurt me so much.

"It's not like she'll be here long—"

"But she is *here*, Roxie," he said, challenging me. He faced me, his nostrils flaring. "She's here when we specifically agreed you wouldn't be helping her again."

He got that wrong completely. *He* was the one who decided I wouldn't be helping Cassidy again and *he* was the one who didn't ask my opinion first before throwing down the ax on the decision.

I shook my head. "You gave me no say in that decision," I said, standing. "You basically took the option away from me."

"But in the end, that was the last of it," he went on, standing too. "In the end, that's where *we* left the conversation, and if you had issues with it then, you never voiced them with me."

I may not have, but I did have an issue with it. That night, I went along with what he said because *he* needed the agreement to be okay with me helping her.

But that didn't mean that I liked how we left things.

At this point, Griffin was pacing, passing me and nearly running a path into our floor.

He faced me. "I don't even know why you want to help her, why you continue wanting to help her—"

"Because I'm human," I admitted, raising and dropping my hands. "Because I have a soul and you know what happened to her at that place she was staying in."

I explained that to him when we made it into the bedroom.

I shrugged. "She needed help."

"And as always you're there to give it," he said, shaking his head. "You give it despite what she did, despite what she put you through. You're not a glutton for punishment, Roxie, so I truly don't get *what* this is."

He wouldn't, would he? He wouldn't get that I had a history before him, that myself and that girl out there knew each other in a life and time well before him. We had so much there, so many things that...

Closing my eyes, I shrank down to the bed. Reaching around my stomach, I massaged as I thought. Cassidy and I did have a history and the truth was, all this?

I was still trying to figure out myself.

It was Griffin that brought me out of my head. He was grabbing his ball cap.

Like he was leaving.

I shook my head. "Where are you going?"

He turned around, his shoulders dropping. "I can't be here while she is, so respectfully, I'm going to go take a drive."

Sighing, he put the cap on his head, straightening. "I'll be back later."

He started to walk away, but I said his name.

Then this.

"Don't rush," I told him, surprising even myself. But he frustrated me.

I frustrated me, too.

The sadness that crept across his face was evident.

And I didn't chase him once he walked away.

Seventeen

ROXIE

IN THE END, Griffin didn't rush. In fact...

He ended up staying out all night.

Worried when I woke up in the middle of the night, and he wasn't there, I reached for my phone to call him.

That's when I saw his text.

Staying with a friend for the night, was all he said and frustrated, I didn't even answer his text. I simply put the phone away, then forced myself to sleep.

It was a restless sleep, active. Between myself and the baby, we were tossing and moving around completely. It was only in the morning when I realized I had forgotten to take Cassidy to a hotel, mostly because she surprised me with her presence.

I found her and not Griffin that morning, the meek woman bundling up a make shift bed on the couch. I thought to apologize for not thinking about her, forgetting her, but in the end, I said nothing.

We stood in front of each other, her and me. She was complete dressed, but I noticed a pair of sleep pants and shorts to the side of an open bag she had on the couch. She brought it in with her.

Fumbling, she turned, stuffing the garments inside before picking up the bags handle.

She pushed some dark strands behind her ear.

"You got a message on your answering machine," she said, pointing to the docked phone near the couch. She shrugged. "The message sound, which is the only reason I heard it. It was a reminder about your Lamaze class today. I couldn't help noticing."

Lamaze class.

I closed my eyes. Griffin and I were *supposed* to do that. In fact...

I checked the time on the back of the docked phone.

We wouldn't make it judging by the time.

Not that it would be a good time for it anyway.

Pushing my hand over my head, I closed my eyes. I stood by my decision to help Cassidy, but this was all turning into a big mess I wasn't sure would be so easy to get out of.

I mean, he didn't even come home.

The reality of that had me sitting down as the soft smell of flowers passed me.

Cassidy was heading away from me, her bag in hand. She turned when I lifted my head.

She smiled a little, a smile I remembered so much that it hurt. We used to be each other's everything once. We used to have so much...

"I appreciate your help," she said, shaking her head. Her eyes glistened a little for some reason, and she wiped them. "But I've overstayed my welcome. I called a cab. I'll be heading out now."

"But where?" tugged at my lips, tugged so hard I nearly said the words.

I swallowed. "Okay."

"Okay," I settled with, *"okay."* It was the only word I basically said to her since she'd come with me the day before.

It was the best I could do.

She gave me an out, my former step-sister, and I knew it would all be over the minute I let her walk out of my home. The exit symbolized her departure from my life. I could let it go. This would *all* be over.

She turned when I called her name.

She was standing in the middle of the living room, her cheeks flushed and her dark hair settling down on her shoulders. Her baby bump peeked out of the simple t-shirt she wore, the shirt not maternity wear in the slightest and since she came back into my life, I'd never seen her actually wearing any properly fitting clothing to accommodate her baby. She probably couldn't afford it.

"Have you ever been?" I asked, my throat dry, burning. I cleared it. "Have you ever been to a Lamaze class?"

I had no idea her history, but I had a feeling she never had.

She shook her head. "No."

Lifting my head, I spoke again. I spoke words I never thought I'd say and probably shouldn't have. Her being her, in my life, had caused so much unneeded drama. She was causing me to fight with my husband and giving me unnecessary stress surrounded the baby. But something made me speak, something made me invite my former step-sister to a Lamaze class, and I had a feeling that something went beyond closure. It was deep.

It was history.

Eighteen

GRIFFIN

A SOFT VOICE and kind eyes brought me out of my head, her smile always inviting. I'd been warming her couch for the last hour or so and, she didn't need to be kind to me, especially since I'd come in unexpected.

I had arrived with excuses, a laundry list full. I just...hadn't known what to do or *who* to go to, but Dr. Dow had entertained me, opening her doors when she didn't have to. I caught her at lunch, her mealtime free of appointments.

Roxie and I had actually done our pre-marriage counseling with her therapist, which was ironic since we ended up getting married before we finished the sessions. We'd done it on a whim, unable to wait anymore. We also wanted to fool the press by messing up the dates of our nuptials. In the end, it worked out. We'd been married peacefully without any media interruption, even with how much had changed since then.

I breathed into my hands, anxious since the minute I filled this poor woman's couch. I barely fit with the extension of my limbs.

"Griffin?"

I swallowed, gazing up to aged eyes. Surrounded by silver

locks, Dr. Dow reminded me so much of my gram, their souls both indescribably good.

She removed her sandwich wrapper from her lap, placing it on the table. I requested she'd continue eating after I'd dropped in on her office doorstep. I interrupted her during lunch, and well, this wasn't a session.

At least it hadn't started out that way.

I literally laid it all out to the woman, my worries about Roxie... everything. I told her Roxie and I had talked that she'd been coming here, that she told me about the sessions, but had been so casual about the detail. I told her I was scared for the well-being of my wife, that a woman from her past had come in, and I had distanced myself in response.

My wife basically told me too.

It all came out like regurgitation, a mess and uncontrollable. But I felt Dr. Dow of all people had been the one to go to. Other than myself, Roxie told her counselor everything. She knew her.

She could help me.

As unusual as it was after Roxie's name had been dropped by me, she hadn't re-entered much into the conversation. I figured that had been confidential. Dr. Dow wouldn't tell me anything about Roxie involving her sessions, and that's not what I wanted anyway. I just wanted some feedback on what to do from a professional standpoint.

I had no idea we'd be talking about me.

She used words like "you," questions surrounding *me*, and all too quickly, I found myself on the other side of the words and in the chair of a counselor.

"Griffin," she started as she sat back and laced her hands across the top of her knee. "Do you ever find yourself feeling stretched too thinly sometimes? I mean, besides this new development with Roxie and even the soon-to-be arrival of your son. Do you ever find yourself being pulled in many directions more often than not?"

I really didn't understand what me being pulled in many directions had to do with anything I presented here today.

And there went another one of those questions, the ones talking about me instead of everything else.

I figured she had a reason for them, though, and I had come to her, the professional.

I leaned forward, opening and closing my hands. "I supposed in the sense that my time is usually tied up, but I wouldn't say I'm feeling stressed or stretched too thin. I always make sure there's balance in my life."

"And you have to balance a lot, right?" she asked tilting her head.

I nodded because she was right.

"I do, but they're all things I enjoy that are both for and involving the people I love. Roxie and her business I fully support. I'm active in it and enjoy doing it. My family business is the same. I'm there for them and do whatever is needed when I can outside of my basketball schedule."

She said nothing after that, simply staring at me.

"I remember you talking about your family and Roxie's during your pre-marriage counseling," she said after a beat, smiling at me. "You all seem really close, you and your family."

"We are. They're my everything outside of Roxie and what we've built. We've had to be there for each other."

"Because of your dad," she cut in, her words, her tone serious. "He had to work, provide, so everyone else came together to make that a little easier for him."

I guess I had told her that back then during marriage counseling.

I shrugged. "It was what it was. My older brothers worked too so I did what I could at home being younger to support the house."

I basically had been the parent at home before we moved back to Texas to be closer to my Gram and aunt. When Colton and I were too young to work, I made sure we did what could be done while my brothers and pop were off to work. I made sure the house was clean, had both my homework and my younger brother's done, all while making sure dinner was ready for everyone when they got home in the evening. We all had our part; mine just happened to be at home.

My family took care of me. Pop and my brothers made sure Colton and I were fed so one day we could go off and pursue our dreams. And now that we had gained the impossible, we could pay it forward.

I could pay it forward.

"And it sounds like you're still doing a lot of that today," Dr. Dow said. "Taking care of everything, everyone?"

I opened my hands. "They'd do the same for me."

"But what if they asked you not to help?" she asked, taking me back a little. She shrugged. "What if they wanted to do things for themselves and for you to step back a little?"

"I don't know," I said, shaking my head. "I guess I'd wonder why."

"Because that's what you need," she said, the words a statement, no question in there. "You need to help. You need to help your family, your dad, your brothers… Roxie. You need to help them all because you care about them. They're your people, your family."

Again she gave me no question. She was telling me something, and it was something I didn't know if I necessarily wanted to hear.

Her legs crossed after she turned in her seat, and that smile of hers continued on, right at me.

"You enjoy helping people, Griffin," she said, her eyes warm. "And I know it comes from a place of love."

It did. It does. I didn't know how *not* to help my family.

I didn't know how not to help Roxie.

In my world, how I grew up, that's how things were. A guy helped out. He helped because that's what his family needed. We weren't like most families. Before my pop, my brothers, and I moved back to Texas and had the help of my gram and Aunt Robin, it had just been us boys. We had no one else, no other parent to fall back on.

My mom had left when I'd been so young I barely even remembered her, but even with no memories, no remembrance of the past, I remembered the absence of her. I remembered she wasn't there and I'd be damned if I let any of my family feel that way about me. I'd always be there for them come hell or high water.

Always.

Closing my eyes, I only came out of my head at the sound of Dr. Dow's voice. She had stood up, came over to me, and took a seat on the edge of her coffee table. She gave me time to crawl out of the space I'd been in—I had been so silent before she spoke.

"It's okay to help," she said, her smile widening. "But like your life, remember to find that balance. Be there when you're needed. Love when you need to."

The wind cut through my hair from the open windows of my Range Rover, the Miami sunbeams rolling over the grooves of my knuckles through the windshield. I drove through downtown Miami traffic.

And I drove unmistakably clouded.

I was in my head, tense. Considering all the doctor said to me in her office, I was left more than thrown.

Her few words had packed quite a punch.

She hadn't said anything flat out, but I could read between the lines like the best of them. She basically told me to take a step back from Roxie, the situation we were in involving her ex-step-sister. That tactic just felt all kinds of wrong, and I wasn't sure that was what I should be doing. I was essentially already taking a step back. I had distanced myself, hadn't I?

I rifled my hand through my hair. I hated that I had put that distance between myself and Roxie last night. She did say what she had and it... hurt. It killed like the worst blade, but despite the fact, I should have risen above it all. I should have fought *harder* and challenged the situation more.

"But like your life, remember to find that balance."

Did I have balance in my life really? Because more and more every day, I was starting to wonder and this only confirmed when my phone buzzed in my pocket shortly after getting on the road.

Lamaze class with Roxie.

It was the second reminder, the first I guess I missed while I'd been with Dr. Dow. The *second* reminder currently displayed on my phone screen and I nearly dropped the device in frustration.

Cursing through my teeth, I slid out of the stream of traffic I was in, heading in a new direction entirely. The clinic we were scheduled to have Lamaze at was about five minutes away. Class had already started about twenty minutes ago, but if I hurried...

I texted on the road, something foolish I knew but I tallied it up to everything else in the last twenty-hours.

Are you at Lamaze class? If so, I'm on my way. Please wait for me. I'm sorry I forgot.

I was sorry for many things. I was sorry I couldn't support her regarding this thing with Cassidy. Though I still stood by my decision, that I didn't want Roxie to help Cassidy in any way anymore, my wife and I should have at least talked about everything a little more. That's how we did things. We talked.

We didn't do what we'd been doing.

I felt more and more like a heel the closer I got to the clinic, the thoughts of everything weighing down on me like a steel blanket. I had no idea if Roxie would even go to this thing by herself, but if she did, I had to at least try to be there.

Pulling into the parking lot connected to the clinic, I barely got my SUV into park before leaping out of it. I ran like the time I spent during ball practice and even quicker when I passed a tiny car.

The Mini Cooper was parked all by itself, lonely with a familiar license plate.

Damnit. She did go.

I went like lightning now, knowing that I was late, but I didn't care. I had to be there. We... We needed to figure out everything that was going on between us. I got in front of the building, sprinting toward the doors.

I spotted her before even making it to them.

She'd been coming out, her purse on her arm. She rustled inside it like she was looking for something and, though I could have approached her, I failed to do so, staying back. She was actually coming toward me, slow and distracted steps in her sandal wedges.

I waited, letting her come. She wore a teal dress that displayed her shapely legs, the material bumping high over her stomach, our unborn child, before falling and swaying over thighs so rich and warm with color. Her dark hair braided singularly, she let it rest on her shoulder during her casual strides, and I wanted to thread the end of it around my fingers, bunch it in my hand while I buried my face in her sweet-smelling neck.

I wanted to tell her that I was sorry, that I should have

been there for her and we could work this all out. Things didn't have to be the way they had before.

She's moving too slow.

I strode toward her then, bracing my hands for the feel of her after I took her in my arms, apologized, but someone else coming up behind her had me stopping once again.

The person came in hot and ironically, out of the same door Roxie had come through.

And they had Roxie's cell phone in hand.

I knew because the phone had a pink case, a distinct case. I drew back, watching what seemed like the impossible.

"Roxie!"

Cassidy waved her arms after the words and wore a dress I felt like I'd seen before. She had it belted, tied above her own baby bump, as she gained on Roxie and the style and design struck me as more than familiar.

Because it was my wife's.

Roxie had... loaned her a dress and she wore it, skipping toward her with my woman's cellphone in her hands.

Roxie shifted at the sound of her name.

And if she didn't look overjoyed.

Her hands rose into the air with surprise as she popped up on her heels a little, a phone presented before her—*her phone.* Upon accepting it, Roxie's smile was evident, and Cassidy herself looked all too the pleased with my wife's reaction. She'd made that reaction happen, made Roxie happy.

Together, the two redirected their steps completely, and I didn't need to be a genius to know where they were heading. Hip-to-hip, they both went back toward the clinic, and I took a seat, the bench for the bus stop close by.

Head in my hands, I forced my fingers into my hair.

I sat there for a long time on the bench, by myself, thinking, but in all that time, it never crossed my mind to go inside.

Because she didn't need me.

Nineteen

GRIFFIN: Do you need time? I mean... to address this thing with Cassidy? Do you need time for it? Do you need to figure it out?

Silence.

Griffin: You do, don't you?

Roxie: Probably.

Silence.

Roxie: Yes.

Roxie: What does that mean if I do?

Silence.

Roxie: Griffin?

Griffin: It means I give you that. I will give you that time.

Roxie: What does that mean exactly?

Griffin: It means I'll be around, but not there, not at the house I mean. If you truly need time with Cassidy, then I think me being there will be in the way of whatever you two need to figure out.

Silence.

Roxie: I don't really like that. In fact, I hate it.

Griffin: It seems best. I think it is best.

Silence.

Griffin: Roxie?

Roxie: Where will you be?

Griffin: With friends. Like I said, nearby. I have a couple obligations out of town, which you probably already know by my schedule, but for the most part, I'll be in the city. Just figure this thing with Cassidy out. Do what you need to do. No need to worry about me.

Roxie: Okay.

Griffin: Okay?

Roxie: Okay.

Griffin: All right. I'll be on standby for a few days, but I'll be there in an instant if you need me, though, if Jackson and you need me.

Roxie: Do I have a choice here?

Griffin: You always have one. Always.

Silence.

Roxie: Okay. I love you. Be by your phone, please. Just in case?

Griffin: I adore you, and I promise I will.

Twenty

ROXIE

"Rox? This is... this is dumb, sweetie."

I knew it was. It was insane, me asking for her to come down to...

Be here with me.

But I was nearing full term with Jackson, my pregnancy just over thirty-six weeks. I was tired. I was *stressed,* and I needed my friend, especially since my other one would be gone for a few days.

I had no idea what this meant for us, Griffin and me. We'd never been so separated on an issue like this. We had always been such a strong and unified front.

He's just trying to do what's best for you.

I knew he was which was why I let him take his time for the next few days. His texts said he'd be around and I could figure the whole thing with Cassidy out. He was giving me space, which was something I probably did need no matter how much my heart didn't want that. I wanted him. I wanted him always.

I rubbed my forehead, my heart and head so conflicted. I almost told my friend on the other side of the line connected to my ear to forget it. I shouldn't have called her. I needed to call my husband, tell him to come home, but her sigh into the phone made me hesitate.

"I'll be there," my friend Clare ended up saying into my ear, finally. "But only because I was planning to come out anyway for the birth."

I knew she was, a lot of people were going to be coming out in the next few weeks.

I hope we'll have it figured out by then.

I rubbed my stomach, my baby, just as unsettled as me.

"Will Destiny be coming, too?" I asked Clare, laying my head against my bedroom wall. I'd come in here to make a phone call.

"She wants to, but she'll be visiting family overseas."

Clare's fiancée, Destiny was second generation Japanese. The two had met while we were in college and recently announced their engagement over the summer. So many changes in all our lives. I would have loved to see Destiny too, have her meet the new baby when he came, but I understood.

I told Clare that was fine, then thanked her profusely for even considering coming down here early in the first place. She said, "no problem," and that she'd always be there for me, but she still didn't like the reasons for which she was coming down.

"Call Griffin, Rox," she said, toward the end of it all. "This separation isn't just bad for you, but Jackson, too. That's his dad and that woman in your house..."

She didn't continue, and she didn't have to. I owed Cassidy nothing, but her being here seemed to be beyond that. It was something else.

I couldn't explain to my friend what, but I did thank her again. She said she'd be on the first flight tomorrow out of town, booking while on the phone with me. I told her I'd be out there to meet her tomorrow, but she told me with me being as pregnant as I was to just hold tight. She'd come to me via a cab.

I didn't have the energy to argue.

I was just glad she was coming and thanked her again, ending the call in the bedroom just as lonely as I began.

God, this is so stupid.

My baby turned in my stomach like that was his way of saying the same.

I lay to my side, curling up on the bed with the little kicker going wild in my belly. I'd turned in early for the night, told Cassidy I hadn't been feeling well, and so much in that statement had been true.

Griffin's texts the day prior threw me for such a loop I had no idea how to respond to them, and I hadn't at first. He sent it shortly after Lamaze class ended, Cassidy and I coming out of the clinic.

But he sent one before that, one that led me to believe he would be coming. In the end, he must have changed his mind, and that left me with who had originally joined me.

Cassidy had done so well that day, had been there despite being pregnant herself. We switched off and on, both learning, and though I thought spending time with her might actually be weird, it hadn't been. It had been familiar.

Eerily so.

The woman had once been my dearest friend, which made it so damn hard when she betrayed me. She truly had broken me, so much and to the point, that I hadn't really been able to have *any* relationships in which I was truly open to another human being for years. Even when Clare and I became friends, I hadn't let her completely in. It wasn't until Griffin.

Everything changed so much with him.

He just wanted me. He wanted me happy, sad, broken... He wanted it all no matter what that entailed. He let me be me with him, standing by my side whether the road was hard or easy. I grew up so much with him by my side. I became the woman I was today, no fear to take the next step. I could be the best mom I could be because I had such a strong support system behind me—with me to the end.

I hugged myself, the bedroom dark and incredibly quiet. I sat in the openness of it, thinking, pondering. The first flashes of lightning brightening up the room sent chills deep into my spine, and the downpour that followed hadn't helped. Thick droplets of rain crashed into my window, and I sat up, the rolls of thunder and lightning pelting down on the house. I got up to close the curtains, bunching up my nightgown, but by the time, I made it back to my bed I lost all hope of sleep.

I wandered out of the bedroom, aimlessly, but eventually decided to get some water.

I kept my steps quiet passing the guest room, not wanting to disturb Cassidy in case she headed to bed, too. I put her up in there, and that's where she'd be staying the rest of her time here.

Clearing her room, I made my way into the living room and would have headed into the kitchen to get that glass of water if not for the storm.

The room filled with light following a clap of thunder, the charged bolt illuminating the room so brightly as if the lights were on. I headed toward the sliding door facing the beach.

But it seemed I wasn't the only one.

Cassidy was already there, her hand on her stomach while she watched the storm through curtained windows. That was why it had been so bright. She'd opened the living room curtains.

Something about the way I traveled toward her took her attention, because eventually, she panned over to me, a small smile on her face.

"Sorry," she said, her hand dropping from her stomach. "Couldn't sleep. Came out here."

She didn't need to apologize. She hadn't done anything wrong.

I joined her, staring out those same windows. So much beauty resided so casually outside of my home. There was beauty in the day, the night, and even evenings such as these.

I rubbed my tummy, the beach and waves still visible through droplets of rain when the sky filled with light. The ocean was inky black, the winds and heavy rain causing the waves to crash hard on the shore.

"Remember when we used to sit outside in them?" Cassidy questioned, her chest bouncing a little when she laughed. "We'd wait for a storm and—"

"Just run through it," I finished, facing her. "Dad thought we were crazy."

"Insane."

"Yeah."

I remembered those times well. We should have been afraid of stormy weather, and most kids were, but not us. We'd wait for those days. Mostly because it concealed us. It concealed our laughter, our screams of glee. We'd run around in them outside my dad's garage, and just well, be kids, her, Radha, and myself.

"Rad would always complain about her hair," Cassidy crooned, ironically sounding so much like her sister back then.

My smile widened. "But she'd always come out with us."

"Always," she chirped, fighting the smile on her own face. "Your dad may have thought we were crazy, but my mom, she—"

She stopped the words immediately, almost at the same time I felt a jolt in my heart.

I did have good times with them *all* back them, all but that woman.

Cassidy and Radha's mom had never been genuinely kind to me. It had been put on and so young, I hadn't realized it at first. It took a long time for me to read between the lines, grow up.

Perhaps, Cassidy knew what mentioning her mom would do, how it would change the tone and suck out any joy from the conversation.

I decided to finish what she'd say.

"She'd yell," I said, swallowing with it. "She'd yell and tell us all to come inside."

Cassidy stared at me, her lips in a hard line. She nodded away from me quickly, and suddenly we were just two women reminiscing about the past. We were two little girls relieving it.

Things went harshly silent between us then, so many unspoken words weighted thick through the air like the heavy raindrops outside. They pressured us both, squeezing so tight to the point of suffocation.

Tired of the lack of air, I bid Cassidy good night. I was so very tired... spent on everything. I'd been playing pretend since the moment I decided to help her out, hardly anything good left around me.

Things had been good, had been happy in my life.

And how I managed to self-sabotage it all.

"Why did you help me, Roxie?"

She asked me the question on the way to my bedroom, my feet heavy underneath me.

Gripping on the hall, I turned, a woman with dark hair still standing by the window. Cassidy had the illusion of raindrops running down her cheeks, the droplets pressed to the glass outside painting her skin.

She held her stomach tight, coming into the light, and those raindrops... they weren't raindrops.

She was crying, crying so hard, and I had no chance to answer her question. She turned away from me, her hand placed on the cool glass.

"I know why," she said, fog creating around her hand. "Because you're good. You're a good person."

I came back a little, watching her, those tears steadily moving down her face.

"You know, I knew about you two," she said nearly whispering the words. She pushed tears out of her eyes. "You and Griffin. I knew you were married, who he was. I've known for years."

I had nearly made it back to her by then, cautious with my steps.

"You said," I started, my voice almost squeaking. "You said... You said the TV told you—"

She looked up at me. "It told me where you were, but only that."

My head shaking, the chills were imminent on my skin, my arms beaded in a thick blanket of them.

What else had she lied about? What else had she led me to believe?

And what didn't I know the truth to?

The possible answers to my unasked questions caused illness to rupture deep within. I had no idea what to do or... or say, but it seemed I didn't need to do anything.

Cassidy's throat moved thickly when she swallowed, her hand sliding down the glass of my sliding door.

"I saw it in a *People* magazine one day," she said, her smile shaky, wobbly. "Both of you on the cover when your wedding photos released."

We had given a few to the press for publication. We'd sprung our wedding on them, left them with nothing. We'd given the photos in good faith, my husband always willing to please the public, such a good man I had.

I sat on the arm of the love seat, staring at Cassidy from the back of the couch. I wanted to say something, but I no idea what.

Her forehead touched the glass.

"I saw him," she said, nodding. "But my eyes... they stayed on you. You were beautiful, stunning in a long ornate gown. You were so happy."

I was happy, so unbelievable happy. It had been the greatest day of my life, and it happened on Griffin's family farm. They welcomed us there, the event completely beautiful.

Dark eyes locked with mine over the couch.

"And I was so happy for you, Roxie," Cassidy breathed, those tears in thick streams. "I was happy you found something, someone."

Her lip pushed over the top of the other, tears falling. Then all too suddenly she turned away, staring at the beautiful storm again.

"It just felt fitting," she said. "Right. You're such a good person, Roxie, and you had good things happen to you. It was right, only right."

She kept saying that, over and over. That it was right, what happened was right, and I got up, going over to her. Those tears steadily fell, and I was so confused, the reason for them unknown.

Her head of dark hair lifted when I made it to her side.

"You know, Curtis and I were arranged," she said, surprising me. "My mom's idea. He had money. Money is good, you know."

She sounded so lost, broken.

Reaching out, I started to touch her, but couldn't... couldn't find my way there.

She used the long sleeve of her top to rub underneath her nose, breathing hard.

"It wasn't long before he started hurting me," she said, her words haunted, eyes empty. "Emotionally... physically."

Oh, my God.

"And I took it. I endured it."

"Your mom. She didn't... Radha?"

I couldn't help interceding. None of this... None of it made sense.

Cassidy faced me after my words, the smile of hers returning when it hiked up the side of her lips. Nose red and eyes puffy, she was still a scathing beauty, stunning like she called me.

"Radha's like a mini version of mom now, Roxie," she said, jaw moving. "She actually laughed when I asked her for help getting out of the situation."

Laughed.

"And mom... she asked me if divorce was the answer. She asked if I could make it work."

Her lips tightened, her breathing heavy and her body shaking. She gripped her arms, looking down and when she did, she pushed a hand over her stomach.

"I endured it all until this," she said massaging her tummy. Her tears fell heavy to the carpet. "I couldn't, not with him or her in there. I refused."

As she shouldn't have... she shouldn't have.

Her eyes grew lost again, then closed so tightly, shutting away her tears.

"I'm so hollow, Roxie," she said, her lips wobbling. "I'm so hollow all the time, and I hate who I am, what I've been. I've followed my mom... my sister, my whole life and I'm so tired of it. I thought I was protecting Radha. I thought I was. I thought..."

Her voice softened into the stormy air, again not making sense. But this time, she didn't continue.

Not until I so deeply needed her to.

She moved when my hand pushed over her shoulder, her dark eyes clumped with tears opening up.

"What do you mean?" I asked, her own words shaky, my throat thick and burning. "What do you mean about Radha?"

She wouldn't say, a stream of tears clipping off when she blinked.

I squeezed her shoulder. "Please. What. Did. You. *Mean?*"

That haunted look took over her brown eyes again. Like she was reliving something, feeling something, and maybe she was.

"It wasn't my secret to tell," she started, head tilting. "It wasn't my secret to know, but after I did, I couldn't leave her. I couldn't, Roxie, and I'm so sorry."

"Cassidy, please." I was crying, the tears hot in my mouth and down my face. I had no idea where they were coming from, but I couldn't stop them.

She attempted to, Cassidy's hand coming to my face.

A warm thumb pushed tears from underneath my eyes, her fingers pressing into my cheek.

"Radha... Roxie..."

I pushed away her tears after her words and her eyes closed, her lips pushing out a breath.

"Radha was raped, Roxie," she said, nostrils flaring with her breath. "She was raped right before we started high school, a boy she started seeing over the summer before. A boy... A boy..."

High school...

The start of...

All that was in my stomach heated up through my throat, my limbs shaking and it took her, Cassidy to keep me up.

She'd change so much, Radha. She'd changed, and I didn't...

I hadn't known why.

I had no idea who had been holding who after the words, just that they had been said and after they had, we were in each other's arms.

Cassidy smoothed her hands down my hair. "Oh, God, Roxie. My behavior... how I treated you. I should never have.

There aren't enough excuses in the whole world no matter how much Radha needed me. I should never have done what I had. I..."

"Does your mom know?" I asked Cassidy, unconcerned about me. The words had muffled by her hair, but somehow she heard me, somehow she found a way.

"She does," she said. "Which was why Radha got anything she wanted, which was why mom hurt you, Roxie. You were so happy, always so happy."

It was all fucked, all a mess, and I... I had no idea what to say, to do.

So I just cried. I cried with a woman. We cried together.

Possibly for each other.

We sat on the couch together that night, more silent than anything else. We didn't need to talk, the air quieting around us both, stillness until there wasn't.

"I'm so sorry," she whispered in the night. She'd been holding my hand, squeezing, squeezing so hard.

My heart hadn't been prepared for it, what she said, and I hadn't even known what to do with the words.

Nor how much my soul needed them.

I didn't respond to what she said. I simply hugged her, holding her.

And those fresh tears hit again.

Twenty-One

ROXIE

THE EVENING FILLED with a woman confessing her soul to me through the night and into the morning. Cassidy hadn't said much more, just what her life had become and why, but never once had she felt sorry for herself. She didn't feel sorry. She felt she deserved every bit of the life she'd made for herself, but it had been I who interceded in those words.

Life... It could be more complicated than some of us could ever imagine. We could be one way, have a lifetime of screw-ups, but it was who we were in the end that mattered the most. It was who we strived to be.

Our pasts never defined us.

The words themselves were something that took me so long to realize, but I was so very glad when I had.

I eventually went to sleep with those words in my head, hugging my child and feeling so warm. I had thoughts of my baby and my husband, my man's arms around us both.

He'd held me all night, never left in my dreams and allowed me such a calm and warming sleep.

His breath in my ear, I shivered at the feel, his calming voice.

"Baby..."

Wrapped up in him, I only let myself bury myself deeper in sleep, taking his strong hands in my mind. I wanted them around me always. I never wanted to leave his embrace.

"Baby, you gotta get up," his voice told me and though, he held me so tight in my head...

His voice was anything but calm.

"Something's wrong," his voice in my dreams said. It urged. *"You gotta get up. It's the baby."*

I woke shortly, ripped out of sleep. I moved around and pulled the sheets away, and found myself in a position I never wanted to be in.

The bed... me... was soaked, my body in a pool, and I didn't understand. I didn't know if it was just coming out of sleep or what, but I didn't *get* what was going on.

It wasn't until the pains started that it hit me.

Twenty-Two

GRIFFIN

"Here on Chicago soil barely two hours and now you're getting back on a plane."

My buddy, D's, hand came down on mine, the pair of us standing outside the airport. He'd driven me here so I could head back home, the need for that an urgency on my end.

In actuality, I was only supposed to be in Illinois *one* hour, but the ceremony... well, it ran late.

Taking my boy's handshake into a hug, I slapped his back, happy as hell for him and damned surprised. But my friend, Diondre, had been nothing but an oddity since I met him in college, so I just chalked today up to the rest of his antics.

My friend had gotten married today, *married* and the evidence displayed before me when he pulled back.

D had on his Sunday best, black and white tux with aviator shades. He topped the outfit off with a gold chain and if he *didn't* have the bling that would have thrown me for one.

I brought my hands down his shoulders.

"I still can't believe you got married," I told him, but his wife in all her glory was sitting right behind us.

In the front seat of his Escalade, Andie sat, donned in a

white, skirted suit due to their surprise nuptials. Apparently, the quick wedding was all they had time for, Andie, a part owner of a nightclub that she couldn't spare too many moments away from. They'd gotten married so quick even our friend Ryan hadn't been able to come out, just me and a few close family and friends. The pair had actually met at the club Andie worked at, his new wife the security detail.

It was a... interesting situation, but the two seemed happy enough, though, and well, she had gotten my boy to settle down.

I slapped his back again. "You keep that one close, okay?" Because not everyone could put up with his arrogant ass.

D's chuckling was boisterous, but it melted a little upon looking at me.

"Things going to be all right?" he asked, those big white teeth of his not showing for the first time since I'd gotten here. "I know you and Roxie are um..."

I'd given him the quick rundown, not long for us to go through everything, but in my heart, I believed Roxie, and I would be okay. That was the only way I felt comfortable going through with coming out here, the event in my schedule for the week.

I gave him a smile I knew to be genuine. My wife and I would be all right, and I wanted him to know. Roxie and I had been through a lot, *dealt* with a lot, and I would readily admit I wasn't always sure I was doing the right thing when it came to her. But this? This space I had given her, I held full confidence in. She needed it. I just had a feeling.

After offering the couple my well-wishes, I was back on a plane, a private one so I could get home quickly. I touched the tarmac in less than three hours and was in my car heading back into the city within minutes. I'd been staying with my friend Kendrick and his wife Kerry for the last couple days, the two very accommodating. My phone rang shortly after getting into traffic, and I patted myself down for it. Roxie's name appeared on the device, and the smile on my face couldn't be measured. I hadn't heard my wife's voice in what felt like eons.

Sliding my finger across the phone to answer, I hoped the separation we had going on was headed quickly to a close.

"Hey, baby. I—"

"Griffin? Hello?"

It wasn't Roxie, and I sat back, trying to decipher the voice.

It sounded like Cassidy, her former step-sister.

I had no idea *why* she had my wife's phone, but I was about to find out.

"What's going—"

"Roxie, it's him. I got him."

Alarm bells went off in my head, my gut turning.

What the fuck is going on?

I had no time to ask, no time to think, or even breathe. Because in the next moment, I got short, labored breathing and I had a feeling it wasn't Cassidy.

"Griffin?"

Her voice sent a shock to the system, but not in the way I wanted. Not like this.

I tried to think, calm my head, as I pressed the receiver hard to my ear.

"Baby," I said moving with traffic again. "Roxie baby, it's me. What's going on?

"Griffin..." she started, but she couldn't get it out. Whatever was up she couldn't say right away.

She breathed. "Griffin, it's the baby. He's coming early."

Jackson...

Jackson.

"Are you at the hospital?" I asked, redirecting that way. "Did something go wrong? Is something the matter? Why did he..."

She said he was early. Why was he early?

"My water," she choked out. "It just broke suddenly, but the doctor said everything should be fine. He said the baby should be okay to deliver, but I need you here. Please. Where are you?"

I breathed a long sigh of relief. Everything was okay. *He'd* be okay.

And she needed me like I desperately needed her.

Charging through traffic, I gave her my location in the city, then asked her all the need-to-know questions—where she was regarding how far along into the labor she was. These were all things we knew backward and forwards, the routine of this day anticipated for a long time, and I said a silent prayer of thanks, I came back home as quickly I did. If I hurried and moved quickly...

I'd be able to help bring my son into the world in person.

Twenty-Three

ROXIE

I couldn't do this without him. He said I could, coached
me over the phone, but I...

Please. Please. We have to wait for daddy.

I called out to my child on the deepest level possible. He
had to wait. We had to wait together for Griffin. He had to be
here for this. It wouldn't be right. He deserved it. He wanted a
child so badly, my rock.

Crying, I couldn't even hold the phone anymore, Cassidy
putting it on speakerphone while I made desperate attempts
to control my breathing and other factors I really had no
control of. If Jackson was coming, he'd come, and he wouldn't
wait for my permission, no matter how much I wanted it.

"Griffin, where are you?"

He told me he was on his way over, in traffic when Cassidy
finally got a hold of him. When he told me all of that, it all
seemed fitting. Like he was supposed to be driving, coming
here to the baby and me.

I got no response from my question, turning my head to
the phone. The timestamp still ticked, but no words from my
husband.

"Griffin?" I called.

Cassidy picked up the phone, here through every minute of my tears and just as scared as I was. My fear went beyond scared, though. I was terrified, and it didn't matter how many classes or books I read to prepare for the day. When one's in the middle of it, experiencing it for the first time and a girl's husband wasn't there to help guide her through it...

"Seconds away," came Griffin's voice, but not from the receiver.

He came into the room, windswept and looking so handsome and perfect. He still had his phone to his ear, a sports jacket in his balled fist. He wore a tie. The reason escaped me at the moment, and the skinny black material hung loosely at his neck. His shoulders broad, he had his big frame donned in a pale yellow button up shirt, the helm pulled out of well-worn jeans.

After dropping the jacket to the floor, he was at my side, his mouth on mine so quick I forgot everything.

The fear, so prevalent before, grew lost, and only he remained, my Griffin. My man and his wonderful smell, my man, and his taste, his love. He held me close, his large hand caging my cheek and I could feel no pain. He managed to dull it, at least for the briefest of seconds. From somewhere in the distance someone told me it was okay. It was okay to push, but I didn't. I couldn't until Griffin's hand came in mine.

He set his phone down on the bed, staring into my eyes and telling me everything would be okay. He swept my hair away, and I spent the next few moments apologizing to him, apologizing for everything that happened and basically sending him away.

He wouldn't hear any of it, though. He told me it was what I needed, that he loved me, and...

It was time to push.

Twenty-Four

GRIFFIN

A MAN'S wife going through childbirth was as equally exciting as it was terrifying. Seeing her go through all that, as well as, her body literally changing and painfully bringing life into the world...

But then there was the aftermath, those tiny fingers, and little toes. There were those eyes that were so new they couldn't even take in light. The room so bright, they closed at first, adjusting, blinking to see and find the world.

To find life.

That's exactly what my son did, Jackson Ethan Chandler. Chandler...

I'd been responsible for that, well his momma and me. We created life. We made a tiny human.

He saw his momma at first when delivered, but that was okay. He should see her first, and his mere existence brought pure joy into her tired eyes, all pain from before gone. I could tell. She saw nothing but him, his tiny, wrinkled fingers reaching and curling in the air.

Roxie kissed one, the smallest digits touching her nose, making her cry.

Hell, making me cry, too.

Roxie looked up at me then, catching me and my slip, but I didn't care. I simply rubbed my eyes and joined her, she and my newborn son with the wrinkled fingers. His skin flushed all over, rosy with a slight brown tint, and I cupped his head, the top of it already filled with tiny brown curls.

He found me then, looked at me then, and wouldn't you know it; he had the bluest, aqua-clear colored eyes. He had eyes like me. Like his pop and in that moment, I realized the importance of that moment.

And how my life would wonderfully never be the same again.

My family looked up when I came out into the waiting room, an intimate area the hospital allowed us to have for privacy purposes. The minute the media caught word Roxie was having the baby, the paparazzi had literally gathered outside the hospital and in some of the waiting areas as well. Those had been the crafty ones, celebrity photographers always on their toes. I had no idea how they found out, but I assumed some of my family might have slipped up and spread the word through their social media accounts. That was okay, though. I didn't mind, as long as the media kept to themselves and let me and mine have this moment. This was our moment, and I was sure that showed all over my face when I arrived in that waiting room to tell them all about the arrival of Jackson.

They pretty much all were there, Pop and Ann, as well as my brothers and their significant others. Poor Colt was all my himself, but he seemed to be busy enough playing with my nieces at the Lego table in the room. Gram joined them, as well as my Aunt Robin. But not just my family was here.

Roxie's friend Clare sat beside Brody's girl Alexa. She'd

been the first to arrive here, apparently already on her way and was located smack dab between Brody and Alexa and my eldest brother Hayden and his wife, Karen. They all chatted amongst themselves, my arrival unknown yet, and in the corner, reading a paper was Roxie's dad, my old Chancellor from college Greg Peterson. Never had I believed we'd all be in a place for him to be here, be active in my wife's life without any heartache or turmoil, but life handed us miracles, handed us blessings.

I pulled the hospital gown off my front, everyone looking up at the sound.

"He's here," I said to everyone really. I smiled. "And mom and baby are doing well. Jackson's actually ready to meet everyone. The doctor said a few at a time, though."

If it were up to me, it would be *one* at a time. It was crazy how a guy was suddenly aware of the possibility of germs and illness when he had a kid. I trusted the doctor's decision, though. And of course, I knew my family would be careful.

I got the expected kisses upon coming further into the room, handshakes of congratulations and tears, and I noticed my Pop's hug went on a little longer than everyone else's exchanges with me. I hadn't been surprised. He'd been that way when Hayden's kids were born too.

"Proud of you," he said to me, his smile tight before dipping his head and I noticed something in his eyes, a sheen before he hid it and placed his hand behind my stepmom's back. Always close to him, Ann allowed him to guide her away, and the pair went toward Roxie's room, my Gram and aunt in tow after I gave them both hugs. My siblings and their girls and the young ones remained out in the waiting room, waiting their turn.

And then there was Roxie's friend Clare.

"She's doing okay, Griff?" she asked me, standing. Apparently, she'd been on pins and needles from what I'd been told, the first to be here.

And boy did she look different.

I'd seen lots of transformations on her end over the years, and today, she'd come with half of her head shaven, the buzzed down hairs tinted blue. She'd always been the adventurous one since I'd known her.

"Perfect," I told her. "She did so well."

Her face flooded with relief, but hiking up on her toes, she whispered something to me.

"And she's out of the doghouse? She'd been giving you a hard time."

I laughed at how she said that, that *Roxie* had been the one in the doghouse and not me for once.

I told her yes, and she gave me a hug. I swear, I'd be all hugged out by the end of everything, and I knew it, so much love in the room. My brothers got me next, as did their significant others, Alexa and Brody last.

"Tiger," Brody said, gripping me in a bear hug hard after Alexa's soft one. Hers had to be soft. She was pregnant as well.

Brody held her after and seeing the two together, I definitely couldn't wait for Jackson to have another cousin.

Alexa put her hand on her stomach. "We can't wait to meet Jackson."

I got that a lot, throughout the whole room in fact. I couldn't wait for them to meet him as well.

I only allowed myself to break away from my family to head over to the man by the window. He stayed to himself for some reason, Roxie's dad Greg I supposed not knowing what to do. He'd folded his paper under his arm, sitting quietly to himself with his hands in his lap.

I decided he didn't have to make the first move or anything else. I went over to him myself, inviting him to see his grandchild first along with the people who raised me.

"There's room for one more," I told him. There'd always be room for him.

Reaching out, I went for his hand and standing, he took it, taking the extra step and pulling me into a hug. Like I said, I sure would be hugged out.

But wasn't that the most wonderful thing?

After patting my back, he pulled something out of his jacket pocket.

"It's Cuban," he said, the thick cigar looking so fine. He scratched his graying, short beard a little. "And one of my favorites."

He didn't know how much I appreciated that, that he was acceptant of me so humbly as the father of his grandchild.

I accepted the cigar, thanking him profusely.

He patted my back, leaving, but I had one more thing.

"Is Cassidy here?" I asked, noticing she wasn't in the room. In fact, she was the only one.

My wife had told me a lot in the quiet of our room, our new baby between us, and I wanted to see Cassidy, thank the woman who helped my wife.

As well as extended an olive branch.

"She was here," Mr. Peterson said, nodding. "But she received a call and went to take it. Maybe five minutes ago? I don't know who it was. I didn't speak to her really when she was here. She sat to herself."

She'd gotten lost in the fray of all this, Cassidy. I noticed her when I got to the hospital, went inside Roxie's room, but after that my focus veered somewhere else. It went to my wife and future child, but I hadn't forgotten who called me and alerted me to Roxie being in labor in the first place. I hadn't forgotten it at all.

Mr. Peterson's hand came down on my arm.

"Is everything all right, Griffin? Should Cassidy have not

been here? I wondered why she was, but as I said, I didn't talk to her."

The reason I was sure had been for Roxie's benefit. He didn't know the whole story, though, and my wife had given me the rundown. Not everything was what it seemed with Cassidy and even her sister Radha from what I understood. I was sure Roxie would tell him everything in due time, though.

After assuring Roxie's dad everything was fine, that Cassidy being here was okay, I excused myself so he could go see his grandkid and I could do my own mission.

"Everything okay, Griff—"

"Fine," I answered Hayden. He had stood up, watching me as I exited our private waiting room.

I met little resistance in doing so coming in the form of two people I worked with quite often, my bodyguards Frank and Joe. They blocked the door from the outside, but when they turned and realized it was me coming out, I only got smiles.

"Congratulations, Mr. Chandler," they both said, then mentioned the calls they'd been receiving from my agent. Deanna had apparently been blowing up their phones for updates on everything. Of course, she was. She cared about my family and me.

"Tell her the baby is healthy and Roxie is fine," I told them, patting their shoulders as I went through their human wall. I thought to ask them if they'd seen Cassidy, give them a description or something for a hint to where she'd gone, but it turned out I didn't need one. Down the hall, she was on the phone like Mr. Peterson said.

And whoever she spoke to wasn't happy.

I knew because the person was speaking just that loud through the device pressed hard to Cassidy's ear and with our private section of the hospital, a tiny cricket could be heard.

"You've embarrassed us," a woman said, very much shouting. The volume actually caused Cassidy to pull the receiver away from her ear, her long, dark hair covering her face. She took the call in a corner, probably thinking the location was remote.

Pulling her hair out of her face, Cassidy returned the phone to her ear. "Mom, come on."

Mom?

Mom.

As in...

"You need to come home," the woman went on. "We saw you all over the television looking a mess."

"We had to rush over," Cassidy said. "Roxie was in labor and—"

"I know she was. Like I said, we *saw* you, Radha and me. You looked disgusting, hair unkempt and clothed messily. And why are you all over Roxie? I wouldn't give you help, but are you really that pathetic enough to ask her? Your *ex*-step-sister you haven't seen in years?"

My first thought had been *damn*, but then my second traveled into the world of *that sounded about right*. Everything coming out of this woman's mouth, this woman who I knew to be Roxie's ex-stepmom was consistent with everything my wife told me about her. She'd been mean. She'd been cruel, and as it turned out, not much had changed even with time.

I thought that remained consistent with Cassidy, but now that I knew the whole story my heart was a little more open. Her past discretions weren't excused at all, not by a long shot but I truly believed there was a decent person in there.

Sometimes they just need the opportunity to be one.

I headed Cassidy's way and so swept up in her call; she didn't turn around.

She cringed. "I wasn't thinking about how I looked. I didn't even see the cameras. Roxie needed—"

"Not you," the woman said. "No one needs you. Now come home."

The call ended without a closing, no "goodbyes" or "I love yous' and never would I have ended a call that way had it been my child.

I guess that made us different people.

Cassidy gripped the phone in her hand, moving her hands on it. When she looked up, she found me and I had to say that I doubted that's who she expected with the width of her eyes.

"Griffin?" she said and actually tried to fix her messy, dark hair up, messing with her shirt. That was the home she came from I guess, that she felt she *had* to do that.

She dropped her hands. "Is Roxie, okay? I mean, she... the baby..."

"Need you," I said, smiling at her, then gestured toward the door my men guarded. "They both do, so if you'd like to go to them, meet your new nephew?"

I guess people weren't so simple, life wasn't so simple. Folks in general tended to make mistakes, but I had never been a guy not to give second chances.

Cassidy watched me, her eyes narrowed like she didn't know what to do with the information she was given, but falling into stride with me, turning back, she decided to roll with it and go with me.

She was on her way to meet Jackson, another member added to this boy's family. He'd have a lot that little guy.

He could never have enough.

Epilogue

ROXIE

A few months later...

"YOU CALL me the moment you get there, okay? I don't want to worry about you."

I would if she didn't. Cassidy was in upstate New York, able to do that after my friend had done the impossible for her.

Cassidy's court case had been tedious and would have been drawn out longer if not for Kerry Donavan's amazing ace attorney skills. Kerry put the pressure on Cassidy's ex-husband, so much that he actually ended up withdrawing his pursuit of their child entirely and actually gave in to a pretty sizable sentiment to boot. This money meant he'd stay away and he signed off on that. As it turned out, he didn't even want the baby and cared less about the money. He just wanted Cassidy. He wanted to own her and have power over her like he had before, and he admitted the fact foolishly. He cornered Cassidy one day, revealed it all, and smart as a whip, she recorded the conversation on a smart-phone Kerry gave her to use when they started working with each other. It had been that piece of evidence that finally made him stay away and well, give my former step-sister her life back.

Former...

Referring to her that way felt so weird after how far we'd come. She'd been very much a part of my life in the last few months, Jackson's. She was his aunt. Even if not legally.

I could almost hear Cassidy's smile through the phone, and even though, I couldn't see her, I knew how much different she looked. She brightened with the day, a glow of a future mama and a *huge* tummy. She was well on track to be bigger than me at my largest, nearly to her third trimester.

"It's something I gotta do, Roxie," she said, content in her voice I was so happy to hear. "But I will call you. Don't worry about me."

I knew it was something she had to do and I wished her well. In fact, I wanted nothing but for her to succeed in her journey.

She was going to see Radha, her intent to try to get her to come around. Apparently, her sister was in a similar situation, a world of physical and mental abuse from her own arranged marriage their mom had set up for her. It was Cassidy's hope she could offer her an alternative and even come back here. Cassidy had a means to take care of them both with her large settlement, and I hoped Radha would take her up on her offer.

She'd already been through enough already.

We *all* had a lot of growing still, and I was aware of that, but if Cassidy managed to get Radha to come around, one day we might even be able to get some of what we had back.

I never gave up hope.

"You take care of yourself," I told Cassidy. "And safe travels. Jackson wants to meet his cousin on time, so you better get back to continue your doctor's appointments."

She had all kinds, both for physical and mental, and she'd

been making great waves. She was getting healthy, on the road to no longer being hollow.

Cassidy stayed quiet for a long time on the line, and I wasn't sure she heard me. But then...

"I love you, Roxie, and thank you."

I loved her, too. I didn't think I ever stopped.

I said as much then hung up the line in my make-shift office. We'd transformed the guest room Cassidy had been staying in before she moved out into a beautiful space with scones and floral wallpaper. It brought the sunshine in, made me happy, and allowed me to get some work done when the baby was sleeping. I wouldn't be working here forever, but I would be during the rest of my maternity leave.

Cassidy had actually moved closer to where Kerry lived, needing her own space, and the baby, Griffin, and I had been frequent visitors.

Speaking of...

Upon leaving my office, I stepped gingerly through the halls of our house, but that didn't seem to matter once I cracked open the door to the nursery.

The sight was... extraordinary, my son and his father. Griffin had taken charge of Jackson while I took time for my phone call, and bless his heart for trying to get our boy to sleep.

Jackson was very much *not* sleeping, his little arms and stubby legs wiggling on his daddy's chest.

And my man...

He was a mass of body, his long limbs spread out on the expanse of a tiny love seat we stationed in the nursery. Griffin covered it entirely and then some, his sleep pants hanging low on his hips and his muscled chest rising and falling with his breaths. Ankles crossed and what looked to be his t-shirt rolled and propped under his neck, Griffin had his eyes closed, his hand gingerly moving across our child's back in small circles.

He was no doubt trying not to fall asleep himself, but our little guy wasn't making it easy for him. He kept wiggling on Griffin's bare chest, and every time he did, blond lashes flew open.

Laughter at the situation, as well as Jackson *and* Griffin's cuteness bubbling in my chest, I couldn't help letting out. I used my hand to muffle it, but I still had Griffin's blond tendrils moving, as he shifted his head in the direction of my position of the door frame.

He frowned at me. "You're amused by this I'm assuming?"

He said it oh-so serious but ended up licking his full lips after his smile. Shaking his head, he lifted his large body with a heave, taking care to hold Jackson tight to him. He waved me over with the tips of his fingers and who was I to say no to an invitation like that?

I came further into the room. "I guess I just find you two adorable."

More than. I could look at these two together all day and have done a lot of it. Griffin was home a lot since Jackson had been born, so much more than he'd ever been. He was by my side, taking care of him nearly as much as I had. We both had to pull together since we'd opted out of formal childcare for the time being.

I knew it wouldn't be our forever. I eventually would need to go back to work, but I'd make it work for as long as I could. We'd been making it work so far.

Griffin's expression danced with amusement after what I said, and he reached up to scratch his fingers against a little bit of the blond shadow he developed under his chiseled jaw. The joys of being a new parent I suppose, but I didn't mind it.

It only made him sexier.

"I'm glad you find us adorable," he said. He pushed a long arm behind the back of the love seat and I took up space right there, the perfect place.

His body warm, I let him engulf me, reaching over to adjust Jackson's little blue onesie. He wriggled, little, chubby brown limbs moving every, which way and Griffin sighed.

He brought a hand down Jackson's back, covering mine and most of our child's small body with his expansive digits.

"I'd be happy if I could just get him to sleep," he said, but he did so with a smile. "He always fusses with me."

"Because he wants to spend more time with you," I told him, pushing my arms around them both. Griffin moved so I could.

I shrugged. "He falls asleep on me, and I can't spend as much time."

Griffin dropped his lips on the crown of my head, making me warm.

"Still, I wish I had his momma's touch," he said, that Texan drawl taking my thoughts to impure places. He made me hot any time he touched me, but his voice.

Knowing we at least had to get our son to sleep, I rose up a little, picking a book from the shelf behind the loveseat.

I came back with it, showing it to Griffin. "You read him this, and we'll both be golden."

I knew for a fact this little boy loved his daddy's voice as much as I did and his eyes were already starting to hang heavy, little lids closing.

Griffin traded off with me, the baby for the book.

I got settled in after that, laying against Griffin with the small bundle in my arms, but my husband didn't read immediately.

He eyed me, flashing a cover with tiny fawn on it at me.

I shrugged. "What? *Bambi* is his favorite story."

We'd knock him out in two minutes flat with this for sure.

Chuckling, Griffin turned it around.

"It's a bit graphic, isn't it?" he questioned, scratching his head. "His momma like dies."

I laughed. "He's a *baby,* and believe me, he'll love it."

Griffin looked unsure, but he did roll with it. Pulling me in close, he let me rest against his chest while he read and I got an even better vantage point, hearing that deep, thick accent from within the confines of his strong chest.

We both stared into a bedroom what seemed like only moments later, a small child sleeping in his crib. His room ended up being beautiful, my former wedding planner making sure our son's digs fared well.

Jackson had a canopy above, opening up and sheltering him like royalty. His mobile of owls, bunny rabbits, and other woodland animals painted shapes on the walls already filled with whimsical designs, his room a wonderland pulled right from a Disney film.

The area was so sweet, like him, and Griffin and I watched from afar at the door at our baby's small body breathing in and out. Having him here was definitely a switch, but never again would I have it any other way.

I leaned back into his father, my man's arms coming in a long expanse of limbs around me. After closing Jackson's door, muscled biceps closed in on me, and at the heat of Griffin's lips on my neck, I sighed, falling back.

He caught me, his hands smoothing down my thighs. My body had changed so much since the birth of our baby. My hips wider and body generally fuller, but Griffin didn't seem to mind the changes I'd been going through.

If anything, they turned him on more.

He gripped me by the waist, causing his cock to hit me in the small of my back due to his considerable height. Hard and hot, his erection was full on, and before I knew it, I was being turned around and guided away.

He only let me walk so far.

In a sweep, he had me in his arms, my sensitive, inner thighs pressing tightly above his hard hips. He pushed a hand along the small of my back, my nightgown so sheer. He took it right off in the middle of the hallway, holding it in one hand while he carried me with the other, my arms around his neck.

He smelled of heat, ocean and I kissed his neck, making him groan and stop in the middle of the hallway.

My nightgown dropped from his hand, and he was pressing me against the wall, my breasts so tender against the solid planes of his chest.

He was like a rock, earth reinforced with steel, and I slid my hands over the firm caps of his shoulders.

He gripped my ass in response, a good bunch in his hands. I only had my panties on at this point, his hot unyielding body between my thighs.

"I need inside you tonight," he said, taking the opportunity to suck on my bottom lip. He drew it in, breathing me, sucking me.

I gasped.

"Are you hurting?" he asked finding my eyes. He was breathy, aroused and I saw that deep in his soft blue gaze.

I shook my head. We'd been having sex for a little bit, post baby, and though, I was fully healed some days could be achy.

I had a different ache, no need for the creative substitutions in the bedroom tonight. I needed *him* inside me, not just his mouth or hands.

Reaching, I found what I heavily sought out, using the back of the wall for leverage, as I grabbed his swollen cock through his sleep pants.

Something of a growl left his lips, his hips swirling and rotating with the movements of my hand. He took my mouth and then he took me, our bedroom just a few feet away.

He pinned me the moment we touched the bed, my arms raised above my head, my body exposed. My breasts were large and bulging, post feeding for the night but still full.

His hand came down on one gently, knowing he needed to

be gentle. He kissed one of my enlarged, dark peaks, his flick of the tongue to my areola driving me wild.

He started slow with his drags, making sure not to go too fast or too hard. He'd take a little and then just kiss, alternating from one breast to the other so neither were neglected.

Dirty blond hairs pushed through my fingers, as I grabbed the back of his head. He was so calculated, so patient and I knew this had to be testing him, his control. This man *loved* my breasts, a one hundred percent and unashamed breast man. Before I'd gotten pregnant, they'd always been his favorite things.

His hand went hot over one, the scratchy stubble of the shadow on his jaw poking my nipples occasionally, stimulating me. He took the scruff against my stomach, my thighs, as he got lower. He pushed his face between them, and he was gone, my leg over his hard shoulder as he ate me out from the inside.

"Griffin... Griffin!"

His beard. It...

Sharp, short hairs pierced my vagina lips, Griffin's tongue moving in and out me. He sucked—hard and at the call of his name, he grinned, his wet tongue sliding along my walls, my clit.

I was drenched down there, and I didn't know how much more I could take. His cheeks hollowed at another suck; his body flushed from labor. I pushed his hair out of his face, and he came on all fours to meet my mouth.

The taste of me donned his lips, him, and the combination took me to a far off place. I could kiss him forever and be underneath him even longer. He had me on his lap when he finally took me, got inside me like he said he needed, and like everything else, he went slow, not wanting to hurt me.

The pleasure on his face I could get drunk off of, him inside me and me a part of him. His eyes actually closed at it, his handsome face engulfed in satisfaction, content. It was like he found peace inside me and I shared the same sentiment.

He fucked me slowly, using both his hips and mine. Eventually, he had me on my back again, pushing my leg up to penetrate deeper, harder, and I basked in every movement, every precise thrust. When he took me hard, it was amazing, but when he had me like this, so soft and loved underneath him...

It was euphoric.

I came with a fury, my walls expanding and contracting around his fullness, and he milked me in response, my arousal coating him below. He watched that, watched me, his hand pushing up my stomach as he rode out the wave.

His abs clenched, Griffin emptied himself inside me, looking so beautiful and perfect above me. I had no idea how I'd come to find this man in my life, but here he was.

And I'd damn well keep forever.

His body came down on me heavy, warm and wonderful. Consumed by it, I curled up on him, and he let me, bringing his arms around me.

We laid for a while like that and not always silent. We actually talked a lot, listened to each other, and those were some of my favorite times. We talked about nothing. We talked about everything and either way, left me in awe of the life I had. I truly had everything and never would I take it for granted.

"Roxie?"

I actually believed he'd fallen asleep, his body still, his breathing even. Turning in his arms, I found Griffin's eyes, bright even in a room only lit by moonlight.

He must have been staring at me too because reaching out, he drew his fingers in a soft line down my jaw, his thumb brushing my lip.

I closed my eyes, enjoying it, then suddenly the warmest mouth made its appearance.

His kiss was different than it had been before. It wasn't for stimulation or even pleasure.

It was just love.

"Baby?" he said, whispering the words above my lips.

I opened my eyes, and he was there, his fingers still floating over my cheek. He brought me in close, and I could tell something was weighing on him, something he wanted to say.

"I love you so damn much."

I hadn't expected that, but I took it, smiling.

I pushed my cheek into his hand. "I love you too so damn much."

The depth of his chuckle I could feel directly from his chest, the sound moving into mine pressed tightly against his.

Tipping my mouth, he kissed me again, and I got to see those soft blue eyes when he pulled away.

"I've come to realize something about myself," he said, smoothing his thumb over my mouth. "That I can't help but take care of you."

I knew that well and found that same quality in myself.

"It's not just you," I told him. "We take care of each other."

Because we did, all the time really.

His lips pulled up into a small smile. "You're right. We do, but..."

His mouth thinned, his jaw moving a little.

"I think it's different for me," he said looking up. He cradled my face in his strong hands. "It is different for me."

"I don't understand. What's different? How so?"

He moved a hand to my hip, strong with his grip. He moved around a lot, restless, and I wasn't sure he was getting across what he was trying to say the way he wanted.

"I've recently been given an opportunity," he started, reaching back and rubbing his neck. "Remember that movie I auditioned for? That script for Roddy Price in Hollywood?"

Boy did I. He practiced for weeks for that audition, myself sight reading alongside him.

I bobbed my head twice in acknowledgment.

"Well, I got it," he said, his lips hiking a little. "Actually months ago. Casting is still underway for other parts and they've been waiting for me, my decision while they finished. That's the only reason I had kept it to myself because I... Because I just don't know yet what I'm going to do."

My initial response had been one of excitement and an urge for congratulations.

Until what he said at the end.

"Well, it's a yes, right?" I questioned, my head tilting. "You do want the part?"

I knew he did. He practiced so hard for it.

He pulled a harsh hand over his head. "What I *want* is beyond the point. There are so many factors to consider. It'd be time away from the baby, you."

"But we'd be okay," I said, pushing my hands to his jaw. "We'd be fine. You could go back and forth and—"

"It'd be months," he went on swallowing. "And time back here would be spent mostly on my day job. Time with you and the baby would be limited."

I understood his concern, but if he truly wanted his role, he could have it. We'd all adjust for him.

I smiled. "It'll still be okay. We'd make do. We have a nanny and could hire another if need be. You wouldn't have to worry about anything not functioning while you're not here."

"But what about me?" he asked, surprising me. His head tipped down. "How would I function?"

I didn't get what he meant.

Nor why his eyes seemed so sad.

It took some massaging, coaxing for him to look up at me, and once he had, it was so hard keeping him there.

His lips thinned.

"I came from a family where a parent walked out," he admitted. "We *both* had parents who skipped out on us, responsibilities?"

What he said was heartbreakingly true. We'd talk about my mom and her decision to take her life when I was young quite a lot since I'd know him, just something that had come up here and there, but something I did notice, was he never talked about *his own* situation not having a mother. I assumed that had just been because he didn't remember her really. She'd left him so young, his entire family.

But maybe I had been wrong that he didn't remember and negligent that he... that he didn't feel.

His heart hammered behind my hand, his long fingers coming over and clasping my wrist.

"And I refuse to be her," he said, nostrils flaring. "I'm not going to skip out on my family no matter what opportunities arise for me. I'm already away enough, Roxie."

"But you and I *both* know it's not like that," I urged, cupping his jaw between my hands. "You're not abandoning us or selfishly pursuing your goals in spite of our own as a family."

"But that's not what it feels like to me." He was serious when he said it, completely. "I need to be there for you guys. It's different for me."

Different...

Different.

And I guess that was why. His *mom* was why.

He'd never shared this with me before, and because he didn't, I had no idea this was a fear of his. But it was, clearly.

I could feel it coming off him.

His lips moved into my hand when I brushed my fingers on his cheek, and I wished I had something to say that could assure what he wanted wasn't a sacrifice of us.

"Remember when I went to see, Dr. Dow?"

His head shot up at my words, his eyes narrow.

Leaning in, I kissed his mouth, smiling.

"I came to her worried," I said. "Actually worried because things were *too* good, too happy. I was anxious because things were too at peace and I didn't know how to deal with it."

Thinking back, the whole thing seemed completely ludicrous. Because something always was going to happen eventually. Something would happen.

But what was the point in worrying until it did?

Griffin's eyes shifted at my admission, but after a beat, a small smile graced his lips.

I pressed my mouth to his. "Do you want this part?"

He let me kiss him, his mouth moving with mine.

"I..." he started, fingers sliding into my loosely pulled up hair. "I can't..."

"Because if you do," I told him, pulling back. "I'm there for you. I'll be there for you and... what if we came with you? What if we weren't apart? What if Jackson and I came along for the ride?"

His brow jumped, his lips parted.

"I couldn't ask you to do that."

I smiled. "Well, I guess it's a good thing you didn't then."

He remained silent for too long, and I knew that brain was thinking, always racing.

"You'd be willing to do that?" he asked, cautiously as if testing out the words. "You'd come with me. Both of you?"

We'd come this far, and we did so together.

I touched my forehead to his. "I can work from home, and I planned to for a little while with Jackson anyway. We'd just be in LA for a while. I could be one of those Hollywood Housewives."

My words caused him to chuckle. He then braced my cheeks, kissing me hard.

"I don't want you to be a housewife," he said, licking my

lips. "I just want you to be you. I want both of you, you and Jackson forever."

I pushed an arm around his waist, sighing as he took claim of my mouth. I just wanted him as him too, and if this was what he needed, I'd be there with him. I would go with him to Mars if he asked me.

I cherished him.

Click the link below to download book six of The Found by You series!

Download on Amazon